BLAZE IN THE STORM

BLAZE IN THE STORM

Aussie Sky Series

Jenny Glazebrook

To my friend from school,

Kristen Bartlett

As a child I was awed by you and your athletic ability.
You seemed able to do anything you set your mind to.
Like so many others, I couldn't help liking
your cheerful, down to earth nature.
As we grew up, I realised that talented or not,
you were on the same journey as any of us.
Like us, you had questions about life that needed answering.
The difference was, you were willing to face life and its questions
with a frank honesty most of us were afraid to have.
With respect and thanks for your inspiration,
I dedicate this book to you
and hope it will answer many people's questions …
or at least give them the courage to ask.

Chapter One

There was something different about today. Bonnie Blake could feel it in the air: cool and alive, it promised adventure. She looked across the hills and shivered. It was almost as though this moment in time was all-important; that someone or something was letting her know life was about to change forever. She shook herself and forced a laugh. Why should life change? She was happy just the way it was. Shielding her eyes against the morning sun, she squinted, then looked harder. There was someone in the paddock next door. He was tall and athletic and he was running with smooth, flowing movements as though nothing could stop him. Even the backpack slung over his shoulder didn't hinder the powerful, graceful strides.

Could he be a school student? No, she would have noticed him at school. He reminded her of a lion or a tiger. She had to find out who he was. Throwing her school bag on her shoulder, she began to run. She was gaining on him, the strong gusts of wind at her back urging her forward. She wasn't sure what she would say when she reached him. 'Hey, I'm a runner myself and I love the way you run,' sounded a bit try-hard. What about 'You run like some kind of animal.' No, that was just wrong. She let out a breathless chuckle. Maybe she should just let him get ahead. Maybe … she stopped mid-thought. A strange sensation began at her feet and made its way right up to her ears. A deep, vibrating rumble. Earthquake, was the first thought that entered her head. But no, there were voices, too. And a cloud of dust that hurtled toward her at alarming speed.

It wasn't until it was almost upon her that she saw what it was. Horses. And riders calling to one another above the sound of the brewing storm.

That was it! The runner ran like those horses – with grace and yet such strength and speed. If only she could run like that!

Bonnie kept an eye on the runner who had also slowed at the sound of the hooves. One of the riders came up beside him and in a sweeping, effortless move, the runner swung himself up onto the horse. Bonnie let out a gasp. Had she really just seen that? She rubbed her eyes. Who were these people? And what were they doing here, racing across her neighbour's paddocks?

* * *

'Hey, look!' Bonnie poked her friend. The principal had entered the geography classroom followed by some new students. The class hushed. Everyone sat up. Bonnie recognised them straight away. Three of the riders from that morning. Even close up they all looked the same: rugged, dark and unkempt. The principal stood before the class, puffed out his chest as though about to make a grand announcement, and then began: 'Year Ten, you have some new classmates.'

Bonnie lifted her hands to give a round of applause, but the principal caught her eye. She let her hands fall to her lap. No point in aggravating him at the risk of being sent out. She wanted to know about these new students.

'This is Prince, Starre and Misty Clements. They and their brothers and sister have just arrived from the circus.'

Well, that explained the runner's acrobatic leap onto the horse that morning. She didn't think Prince was the runner, though. Were they triplets? Bonnie looked from one pair of large, dark eyes to the next. They had to be. And they looked as though they had stepped out of the circus right that minute. Prince looked just like a Prince, tall and regal. His name suited him from his dark, wavy hair, down to his riding boots covered in dried mud. Starre looked as though she was made to perform. Everything about her spoke of grace and poise. She even wore her riding boots with style. Misty was different. She wasn't as beautiful as her sister, but she had permanent dimples which gave the appearance of a continual smile. There was a large rip in her ragged shirt and a graze across her cheek. She met the students' curious eyes and smiled. She wasn't likely to have much trouble making friends with a smile like that.

Miss Sanders seemed strangely lost for words as the principal left. 'Ah … I'm Miss Sanders. Um … if you just … if you'd like to take a seat?'

The triplets went to find somewhere to sit, and Bonnie noted they moved like cats on a paling fence. Each step was silent, stealthy and careful. The dimpled Misty glanced around the room. Her eyes met with Bonnie's and stopped. With a warm smile, Bonnie moved over. Bradley invited Starre to sit with him and looked delighted when she did. He moved closer, invading her space.

'So, are you named after a horse or what?'

Starre's eyes narrowed and she gave him a look of contempt. Bonnie shook her head in disgust at Brad, then looked directly at Misty beside her.

'I'm Bonnie, and that boy there with no manners is Brad, our principal's son. You'll soon learn to ignore him.'

Misty's dimples grew as she smiled. 'It's okay. We get asked that a lot. The truth is, we were named after horses.'

Bradley chuckled from behind. 'Misty like that race horse called Misty Morning.'

Bonnie spun around. 'You're not included in this conversation, Brad. Mind your own business!'

Bradley glared at her before turning his attention to the circus girl beside him.

Class began and Misty took a chewed pen from her top pocket. 'Where's my paper?' She began rummaging through her bag, which smelled very strongly of horse.

'Here's some paper.' Bonnie turned around and grabbed Bradley's note book from his desk, tore out a few pages before he could stop her and then threw it back at him.

'Hey,' Bradley yelled, while Misty held out a rather dirty hand and took the paper from Bonnie. Immediately the clean, white sheet was covered with brown fingerprints.

'Miss, Bonnie just tore up my notebook!' Bradley waved the remnants of his notebook in the air for the whole class to see.

'Bonnie?' Miss Sanders questioned.

'Yes?' She looked up, her blue eyes wide, and she hoped, innocent.

'Bonnie, I'm getting very tired of hearing the same thing day in, day out—' Bonnie didn't let her finish.

'I was just helping the new student, Miss.'

'By tearing up Brad's notebook?'

'He wouldn't have written anything of value in it, anyway, Miss.'

Brad swiped at her with his book. Grinning, she grabbed it from his hand and hit him over the head. He ducked and the class burst out laughing. As the disturbance died down and the amusement subsided, Bonnie sat quietly, knowing what Miss Sander's next words would be.

'Bonnie, please leave the room.'

She stood up. 'Now?'

'What do *you* think?'

Purposely, Bonnie ignored the teacher's sarcasm. 'I think it would probably be to your advantage if I did.' She flashed a roguish smile. 'After all, this is an important time for you, developing relationships and making a good impression on the new students and all. And my presence seems to bother you, so perhaps …'

'Get out, Bonnie.' Her voice was now low and sounded so tired Bonnie took pity on her and left the room. But she grinned again and snatched Brad's ruler from his desk on the way out. Being the principal's son was enough reason to harass Brad.

Miss Sanders sighed. 'Leave the ruler.'

Bonnie threw it back at Brad and left again, the laughter of the students following her. Standing alone in the corridor, she grew bored, longing to go outside in the brewing storm. She scratched a finger nail along the bricks until curiosity got the better of her. Quietly, she sneaked up to the classroom door and waved to Belinda who could see her from across the other side of the room. Belinda grinned and looked down. However, Bradley noticed her too.

'Miss, I can see a little mouse head peeping around the corner.'

The 'mouse head' pulled a face at Brad before disappearing. She was planning to peep around the corner again when her Uncle Bill strode down the corridor on his way to class. He slowed down when he saw her and rolled his eyes.

'What for this time?'

Bonnie just grinned and batted her eyes at him. Having her uncle as deputy principal in the school was a great advantage. He shook his head then sighed, though she knew he wasn't really upset.

'I suppose you might as well come along with me and learn something.'

Bonnie nodded and fell into step beside him. The Year Twelves working in Uncle Bill's Art class looked up and a few chuckled when they saw Bonnie for the third time that week.

'What did you do this time?' someone called from the back of the room.

Bonnie shrugged. 'Not sure exactly. Maybe I bothered Miss Sanders while she was trying to make a good impression on the new students.'

'What did she do, Mr Richardson?'

Uncle Bill ignored the student's question and gave Bonnie a gentle shove. 'Go and complete your art piece and don't bother me while I try to make an impression on *my* new student.'

'Complete?' Bonnie threw him a grin. 'I don't think complete is quite the right word. I haven't really started.'

Students moved over to make room for Bonnie to set up her work but her attention had been caught by the figure across the other side of the room. There was something about him; even bent over his sketch pad she thought she recognised him. The runner.

She lowered herself into a seat. 'So you've got a new member in your class.'

The student beside her nodded. 'Yeah, that's Blaze Clements, older brother of the triplets and twins.'

'There are twins as well?'

'Yeah. Storm and Beauty. I haven't seen Beauty, but Storm's name suites him. He looks like he has just been out in a storm. Needs a decent haircut if you ask me. Hair all over the place.'

Bonnie nodded, but she wasn't really listening. She was still studying Blaze.

The student chuckled. 'If you're going to take a liking to one, I've heard his brothers are a lot better looking. Not that anyone knows what Blaze looks like, anyway. He's been bent over his work since he got here.'

Bonnie didn't answer. Maybe Prince was better looking, but there was something about Blaze. Something about the way he ran, something about the way he had leaped onto that horse, and something about the way his dark hair now flopped over his sun-browned forehead. She felt drawn to him in a way she couldn't understand.

'You're being emotional and irrational,' she chastised herself, tearing her gaze away and trying to focus on her work. She had painted the family car last week, but unimpressed, had soon thrown it out. She needed something alive. Something moving. Suddenly a vision of the horses she had seen that morning flashed through her mind. She set to work with a slight smile, resolute.

Finally she stood back, 'Oh no ...'

'What's wrong?' Uncle Bill came over.

'It looks like ... I don't know what it looks like!'

Uncle Bill studied the painting for a few moments, eyebrows raised, his mouth twitching. The students laughed outright.

'It's a dog,' one guessed.

'No, it's a goat,' said another, while Bonnie just groaned. The bell for recess went and the class began to leave, laughing at Bonnie's effort as they filed past. Bonnie, however, was determined not to leave her painting as it was.

'The neck should have more width.'

Bonnie turned at the unfamiliar voice. She met the dark eyes of the new student, Blaze Clements.

'It should?' Bonnie tried not to stare. He was the runner. It was definitely him. She could tell by his stance; the way he moved.

'Yep.' He relaxed as he turned his focus to the painting and took the brush from her hand.

Uncle Bill smiled, 'Well, can I leave you to fix it for her,

Blaze? I want to go and grab a cuppa from the staff room.'

Blaze chuckled. 'I'll try, but I can't make any promises!'

He began moving the brush in expert strokes across the canvas. He even painted like he ran – with those strong, flowing movements.

"So haven't you seen a horse before?'

Bonnie was fairly sure there was teasing in his tone.

'The trouble is I have no idea when it comes to actually putting things on paper.' She was studying him out of the corner of her eye. He wore riding boots and ragged clothes just like his brothers and sisters, but he was different. That face was covered in pimples. He didn't have their smooth, unblemished skin. It was true his face was not a display of rugged perfection, but she knew there was much more to a person than their looks. Besides, there was charisma and intensity about him that drew her.

He chuckled again. 'So you're not on friendly terms with paint brushes?'

'Give me the real, living creature any day!'

Blaze grinned, his eyes still on the board as he tried to adjust Bonnie's work. 'You'd fit into my family just right. You sound just like Johnny.'

'Who's Johnny?'

'My dad.'

He called his father 'Johnny'? 'Doesn't he like drawing either?'

'He likes nothing but horses.'

She straightened, intrigued. Clearly Blaze was more willing to share his personal details than the rest of his family. 'What about your mum? Do you call her by her first name, too?'

'Amy? Nah.' He dipped the paintbrush carefully in the paint. 'Not that I remember anyway. She died when the twins were born. I was only little.'

He seemed so at peace with the fact, that Bonnie couldn't

help staring at him. What kind of people were the Clements?

'It's okay,' he said, as though reading her thoughts. 'Everyone in the circus is – I mean was – our family. Plenty of mums to go around.'

He glanced at her and she tried to alter her shocked expression.

'We grew up in the circus,' he explained as he turned back to the canvas and continued work. The picture began to magically transform into a horse. 'But Johnny has decided we need to concentrate on our education now. He thinks being in a classroom is better than learning by correspondence.'

Bonnie watched him as his careful strokes skilfully brought the horse to life. 'You don't seem to have any education problems.'

'Maybe not in art.'

'You'll do great in PE too.'

'PE?'

'Physical Education. We get to run, play sport …'

His dark eyes lit up. 'That's a subject? How can they mark you on that?'

'Oh, they manage. But life's not all about marks, you know.'

He grinned. 'Obviously. Otherwise you'd try not to get yourself thrown out of class so often.'

She looked sheepish. 'You know about that?'

'I'm not deaf.' He gave her a meaningful look and she felt her heart race. Had he heard her talking when she first arrived in the room? Had he picked up on her interest in him?

'I'm not going to find school quite as difficult as the triplets and twins. I've done a lot more reading.'

'You had time to read while working in a circus?'

'Once horses stopped being the reason I lived and breathed.'

'So what's the reason you live and breathe *now*?'

Blaze smiled again and she liked him even more. 'I'm going to be a minister.'

'Prime minister?'

'No, a church minister.'

Bonnie's eyes popped open. 'You're kidding! Like a priest? I've never heard of a circus boy becoming a minister of religion!'

Laughing, he put up a dirty hand and straightened his collar. 'It would suit me though, wouldn't it?' He cleared his throat and assumed a pious expression.

'The circus suits you better. Have you considered being a clown instead?' It amused her that a circus boy would consider being a minister of religion. It was as unlikely as a vegetarian working in the local abattoirs. She chuckled at her own thoughts. 'Hey, why did the cow take itself to the abattoirs?'

Blaze looked startled by the joke out of nowhere, then slowly smiled. 'I don't know. Why?'

'It was attempting to commit silverside.'

'Where'd that come from?'

She poked him. 'Come on, it's funny. Silverside comes from cows ...'

He laughed, then. 'I know, but we were talking about ministers and the circus and then you just come out with this thing about cows.'

She shrugged. 'Yeah, sorry about that. Where were we? Circus ... religion?'

'Plans for the future. Your turn. What are your plans?' He returned his eyes to the painting and she knew that more than anything she wanted to get to know this intriguing circus boy better.

'I dunno. I'm too busy living to have time to think of the future.'

'Too busy living?' He adjusted her painting some more. 'Surely you must have some plans, though?'

'No, plans spoil things, especially if they don't work out.'

'But you can dream, surely?'

'Who needs to dream? Life's pretty good as it is, I think.

Dreams are for the discontented.'

Blaze stopped painting and turned to her, his look warm and friendly. 'You are a cheerful, unrefined character, aren't you?'

She didn't know what he meant by unrefined, but his tone and expression told her it wasn't an insult. She made no comment as she stared at the painting of the horse before her. It was galloping across a stormy paddock and looked as though it were really moving. If only she had that ability to bring a picture to life. If only she could make a horse look like a horse!

As Blaze left for the Year Twelve common room, he turned back and called, 'Hey, unrefined girl.'

'Yeah?'

'I forgot to ask your name.'

'It's Bonnie.'

'See you around, Bonnie.'

As she watched him go, she smiled. Blaze Clements was the unrefined one. She'd never met anyone quite like him before.

Chapter Two

A few days later, Bonnie looked out into the crowd filling the school library. Her next words would determine victory or defeat for her debating team.

'I don't believe violence can be controlled by violence!' She was using what Belinda called her intellectual voice. Hands on hips, she allowed her eyes to meet with as many of the audience as possible. Wide and innocent wouldn't work now. She needed challenging, confident. Still friendly, but in a knowing way.

'It's like forcing someone to swallow disinfectant to cleanse them of the poisonous chemical they have just consumed. It doesn't make sense. It just compounds the problem. Maybe meetings sound dull and tiresome, but believe me, compared to the sound of gunfire and cries of grief, a peaceful meeting is the sound of heaven. And if that meeting contains the sound of snoring, that too, is the sound of life.'

A chuckle rose from the audience and Bonnie sat down to a round of applause. Belinda was smiling wide. 'Well done! I reckon we've got them!'

The adjudicator stood, amusement creeping across his face. 'We will have the results shortly. Feel free to talk among yourselves for a few minutes.'

Bonnie's gaze swept the audience. There was Sarah May and even Rachel Seton. Rachel usually spent her lunch times practicing the piano in the music room. Beside Rachel was Blaze Clements. When he looked up and caught her watching, he shook his head, a twinkle in his eye. She grinned back, and then turned to see the judge's door opening. Silence fell over the room, waiting for his announcement.

'The Southern Plains debating semi-final has been won by Everdeen High.'

The audience erupted into yells and shouts of victory while Bonnie smiled in pleasure at her team mates. They had done it again.

As they left the library, Bradley faced the group. 'I can't debate anymore.'

Bonnie turned on him. 'What do you mean? We have our final tomorrow. You can't back out now!'

'Just watch me!' Brad gave a challenging grin, and then became serious again. 'I have my soccer finals tomorrow, too. I have to make a choice. And Dad decided last night that I have to choose between soccer and debating because he reckons doing both is affecting my school work.'

Bonnie frowned, 'Your father wouldn't know what's affecting anybody's school work. All he does in this school is collect the mail, and then sit in his principal's office reading it.'

Brad grinned good naturedly at the comment which she had intended to be offensive. 'Well, you ought to know. You spend enough time in his office.'

'I do not!' She swung her folder at him then brightened. 'Don't worry. We'll find someone else. I mean, after today's victory, who wouldn't want to join us?'

Belinda rolled her eyes and groaned. 'Get real, Bonnie. No one will want to join us.'

'Of course they will. Why wouldn't they?'

'Because nobody can live up to what you did today. Nobody else in the world can talk like you do. And the final is tomorrow. There's no way we can find someone in time!'

'Come on, Belinda!' Bonnie laughed at her friend. 'Don't be so down. You're always gloomy after a big win.'

'I'm serious, Bonnie. You can try to find a new member, but I haven't got the time.'

Bonnie shrugged. She would do just that.

* * *

'Hey, watch out Lightning. I'm coming through.'

Bonnie turned to see who owned the voice calling out to her. She normally escaped out the school gate and began her run home well before now, but thanks to another of Brad's disruptions the class had been kept in late. Horse hooves pounded toward her. The rider was one of the Clements. She knew it had to be young Storm. His wild mop of curly black hair blew in all directions.

'Lightning? What's this Lightning business, Scruffy?' Bonnie yelled back as he flew past on his horse. She grinned as one by one the twins, then the triplets passed her with a shout.

Belinda was watching with something close to a sneer. 'Why do they all love you and hate everyone else?' She shook her head. 'They would do anything for you, but they won't even talk to the rest of us.'

Bonnie laughed, but in her mind a plan was beginning to form. Would the Clements family really do anything for her? Perhaps she could find someone among them to join the debating team. She glanced around and saw Blaze striding toward the school gate.

'Blaze! Wait!'

He stopped and looked back. His smile was warm as he reached her. 'Who's that yelling in the wind?'

She grinned. 'Just a helpless maiden in need of rescuing.'

He raised an eyebrow. 'Well, you called out to the wrong one. Prince Charming has already ridden past on his royal horse. I can't even claim to be a knight in shining armour.'

Bonnie's grin stretched, while Belinda's eyes widened in disbelief at the banter. 'I can't believe I just said no one else in the world can talk like Bonnie!'

Blaze gave her a quizzical look.

'Ignore her.' Bonnie took his arm and drew him a few steps away. 'Now here's my proposition. I can't make you into Prince Charming, but I can help you gain the title of knight. In fact, I could make you into a real hero.'

'Yeah? How?'

'We need another champion for our debating team.'

Belinda gave a snort and stalked off while Blaze's eyes showed his concern. 'What's up with her?'

'She doesn't believe I can find another member for our team.'

'Well, you do seem a bit desperate.'

'Desperate?' Bonnie was indignant. 'I'm not desperate!'

'You are. I mean you just asked me, someone you hardly know, to join the team.'

Bonnie frowned. 'You don't need to know someone that well to know they'd be good at debating.'

'You need to at least have heard them debate, though. You need to know they can hold an argument.'

Bonnie tried to suppress the grin now threatening to split her face. 'True, I suppose.'

'And you've never heard me ...' A slow smile began to form as his voice faded out.

'I've never heard you debate?' Bonnie finished for him with amusement in her bright eyes.

He let out a laugh. 'Until now,' he agreed. 'All right, Bonnie.

You win.'

'Not until you join the team, I don't.'

'I'll join.'

A satisfied smile spread over her face. 'Thanks. This distraught maiden's countenance has miraculously lifted.'

He chuckled. 'And I get to be the knight without a horse?'

'You don't have a horse of your own?'

'No.'

'Well, you can still be a knight, but I won't kiss you until you get a horse.'

Shock showed in Blaze's dark eyes and Bonnie saw the blush filling his cheeks. He cleared his throat and pulled at his collar. 'Well, we'd better head home.'

Bonnie nodded, realising she would have to tone down any flirting. It obviously made him uncomfortable, and the last thing she wanted to do was drive him away.

The two walked in awkward silence while Bonnie searched her mind for something to fill it. 'Hey, didn't you say you want to be a minister?'

He nodded.

'Well you'll be a great help in tomorrow's debate. The topic is "That the devil is a myth".'

'What?' Blaze looked incredulous. 'What kind of a debate is that?'

'A good one. We're on the affirmative, but you must know enough to be able to slam their arguments even if you agree with them.'

Blaze said nothing and Bonnie stopped to look at him. 'What? What's wrong?'

He shook his head. 'Sorry Bonnie, I have to back out.'

'Huh? Why?'

He looked anywhere but at her. 'I just have to.'

'But why? What's happened?'

He looked at her out of those intense dark eyes and Bonnie couldn't draw her gaze away. There was something deep going on here; something beyond all she had known. He obviously didn't want to share whatever was going on with him right now, but she had to know.

'Come on,' she pushed. 'You can't back out on me like that with no explanation.'

Blaze sighed and she had to move closer to catch his quiet words. 'I, well, I just can't argue for something that is so wrong.'

'But Blaze, that's what debating is about. You can't get involved personally.'

'I know.'

'So what's the problem?'

Blaze started walking again and it seemed he wasn't even going to answer. She grabbed his arm. 'Come on Blaze, explain this to me. I don't get it.'

He shook his head sadly. 'It's all happening again, Bonnie. This happened in the circus, too. My faith in God makes me lose friends … it always causes so much trouble. I just don't want to talk about it.'

Intrigued, Bonnie wouldn't let him leave it at that. 'But Blaze, I'm asking you about it. I really want to know.'

He studied her, looking thoughtful, then shrugged. 'I can't be involved in this debate because it really is too personal for me. Believing in God and knowing the devil is real is a matter of life and death. I just can't ignore my beliefs like that.'

'Oh no,' Bonnie moaned as she covered her face with her hands. 'How can my knight have fallen off his horse when he doesn't even have one?'

Blaze laughed at her dramatic expression, and then sobered. 'I'm sorry, Bonnie, but going into that debate would be like being on the opposing team to you today, when my family had all been innocent civilians killed in cross-fire. I just couldn't argue that violence was a way of gaining peace.'

Bonnie thought on his words, and then raised serious eyes to his. 'It means that much to you?'

'More. It would be like …' He paused and looked thoughtful. 'Like being on the Titanic and knowing it was sinking but arguing everything was fine because I wanted the passengers to enjoy their trip – and then escaping in a life boat without them.'

Bonnie's mind boggled. If only this incredible Blaze Clements would be on the debating team! He had real potential. But obviously his God meant too much to him.

'Okay.' The sparkle returned to her eyes. 'I'll find someone else to join the team, but Blaze, if I seem interested in your beliefs you should know it's only because I want ideas for arguments against the other team!'

They walked in comfortable silence until they came to the lane leading to Collagg's waterfall. Blaze turned to Bonnie. 'This is my stop.'

'You live here? There's no house on this block – just a waterfall.'

'And stables. And our caravans. Come and have a look.'

Feeling cautious, she followed him up the lane.

A round, balding man waved at them across the paddocks as they approached. 'Hello kids! Is this the Lady Lightning I've heard about?'

His voice bellowed with a force that made Bonnie cringe. How could somebody be so loud?

'That's Johnny,' Blaze explained, not bothering to call back across the paddock to his father. 'The triplets call you Lightning because we see you running to school every day, and you're so fast.'

Bonnie dismissed the compliment, focused on her purpose.

The moment Misty, Beauty and Storm approached from their various caravans she began her spiel.

'We need another member for our debating team at school. I don't know if you were there today, but we won.'

Storm grunted unenthusiastically, shaking the mop of hair from his eyes. 'The whole school was going on about that victory as if nothing could be more exciting. You'd think Everdeen has never won anything before.'

Bonnie immediately ruled him out. She faced Misty. 'What about you?'

Misty avoided her eyes. 'Ask Starre. She gives anything a go.'

Bonnie looked around but couldn't spot Starre.

'What's wrong with Blaze being on the team?' Storm demanded, his voice gruff. 'He's the one who wants to be a minister, so he needs to learn to waffle.'

Bonnie tried not to smile at Storm's comment. 'He can't. We're debating "That the devil is a myth".'

'So?'

Blaze bit his lip. 'I can't be part of a lie, Storm.'

Storm scowled at his brother. 'Oh come on, stop being so serious! It's just a debate.'

Blaze fell silent and Bonnie looked around again. It appeared Blaze was the only one in his family who took religion seriously. The last thing she wanted was to cause trouble for him.

'Don't worry about it. I'll ask Starre.'

Blaze went to get Starre for Bonnie and she was left smiling around at Storm, Misty and Beauty.

'So, you're not all horse-crazy people, then?'

'Blaze isn't anymore,' Misty dimpled. Then she sobered, 'But he was sad to leave the circus, too.'

'So why did you leave? Blaze said it was for your education or something.'

The three looked at one another as though a secret passed between them. Storm lost all arrogance as he met her eyes. 'We left because it's safer here.'

'Safer?'

He nodded. 'It's true that Johnny wanted us to get an education, but Marcos, the circus owner, wanted our horses so badly he would have tried anything. That's the real reason.'

'Why did he want your horses so badly?'

Storm gave Bonnie a look of reproach for needing to ask. 'They're thoroughbreds and they're the best trained horses in the country.'

Bonnie smiled at the confidence in the boy's voice. 'Didn't *you* train them? Why didn't he want you instead?'

'He did. He wanted a life-time contract with us, and when we wouldn't sign, he didn't pay us for weeks. Then he said he would kidnap Starre if we didn't give him one of our horses.'

Bonnie's eyes widened in disbelief. 'So what happened?'

'Blaze gave them Elle Ripple.'

'Elle Ripple's a horse?'

'Yeah, Blaze's horse. It was awful when he gave her up but he reckons our lives mean more to him than his horse. None of the rest of us could have done it.'

'Seriously?' Bonnie was totally taken aback. Misty confirmed Storm's story with a nod and Bonnie wondered what kind of people would value the life of a horse more than lives of family members.

Blaze and Starre were wandering across the paddock to where Bonnie waited.

'Blaze told me about your debating team,' Starre said quietly. 'I'll give it a go.'

'Great!' Bonnie smiled back, trying not to stare at the streak of dirt down the side of the girl's face. Perhaps she would have to teach Starre a little hygiene before they began on the debating. She was about to head home when Johnny arrived from the paddocks. He held out a chubby hand for her to shake. Gingerly, she did.

'Good to meet you, Mr Clements.'

He let out a loud laugh and she blushed. 'My, she's a proper lady, isn't she!' He looked her up and down, beaming as though she were a joke. 'Proper manners, clean hands, tidy clothes … not a hair out of place.'

With an uncomfortable smile, Bonnie told Starre she would be back later to help with the debate, excused herself and headed home. She heard Johnny's comments about her appearance following her all the way to the gate.

Chapter Three

Bonnie returned to the caravans that evening, arms laden with books. She dumped them unceremoniously on a log, then sat. Starre sat beside her and stared at the pile, clearly not knowing what to think.

'So we've got tonight and tomorrow morning to get as much information as we can.' Bonnie placed a book in Starre's lap and grinned across to where Blaze sat a few metres away. 'And we're in the perfect position to be able to do that!'

'We are?' Starre looked dubious.

'Of course. We have Blaze's knowledge right at our fingertips. We just find out what he believes, then work out arguments against it.'

Blaze looked up from the book he was reading to meet her mischievous look. She was provoking him, but planned to do exactly what she threatened.

Starre wrung her hands. 'You know, I'm not very good with words.'

'Don't worry about that. We'll put you first, and all you really have to do is define the topic and make a few points.' She saw Blaze's look and gave him a reassuring smile. 'It's okay, she's going to do well in this debate.'

Blaze frowned. 'I know.'

'So what's up?'

He hesitated before answering. 'I guess I'm just not sure it's good for her to be in this debate, either.'

'Why? She doesn't believe what you do, does she?'

'No. But … never mind.'

Chuckling at his concern, Bonnie threw a screwed up piece of paper in his direction. 'For someone who doesn't want to debate religion, you sure look like you want to!'

A smile broke his serious look, though it was clear he fought it. 'I know. It just means so much to me.'

She nodded. 'I can see that. Well, I guess you won't be helping us with this debate tomorrow.'

'I hope not! Not if anyone believes what you're saying, anyway.'

Despite his strong beliefs, Bonnie found Blaze Clements appealing. Something about his intense eyes and serious expression made her long to make him smile. He didn't think or speak like a normal teenager, but then, neither did she. Her thoughts were interrupted as Johnny's bellowing voice came across the paddock.

'Hey kids, why not show Lady Lightning what you can do?'

It took a lot of convincing for Storm and Beauty to agree to perform their circus act for Bonnie, but the rest seemed keen to show her what they had spent their lives doing. Bonnie was amazed as they stood on the backs of moving horses, balancing on one leg, and then even on their hands. They jumped from one cantering horse to another, urging them to a gallop. They made it look so graceful and easy, but Bonnie knew it was extremely dangerous. Each move was performed with confidence, grace, and poise and she watched in awe, her mouth open.

'What do you think?' Johnny was obviously pleased with

his family and their performance and stood beaming at her, pride in his voice. Bonnie searched her mind to find a word to describe what she was thinking and feeling. She didn't usually have trouble with words, but right now they were eluding her. Finally she shook her head.

'They're all … well, just unbelievable!'

Blaze slowed each horse, allowing the riders to nimbly jump down.

'Misty put me off balance again,' Storm growled as he came over.

Starre turned on him. 'Shut up and forget it, Storm. We're not performing anymore, so it doesn't matter.'

Storm glowered at his sister. 'Well, you wouldn't know it. If that wasn't a performance, what was it? Just plain old showing off? Or do we have to show Lady Lightning we're good at something too – she can run, we can ride?'

Bonnie glanced at Johnny who seemed totally unconcerned by his son's attitude. He was ignoring Storm and grinning at her.

'Quite impressive, aren't they.' It was a statement, not a question.

'Unbelievable!'

* * *

Starre's anxiety was obvious as she stood before the school the following afternoon. This was the final debate and the library was crowded. Starre scanned the room and then turned to Bonnie. 'What if I mess this up?'

'It won't matter. Belinda and I come after you and we'll pick up the pieces.'

Starre's watery smile was not convinced as she slowly stood and faced the other team. 'For a start,' she told them, her voice shaking, 'our definition of devil will be different from yours, because "devil" is the epitome of "myth".'

Bonnie grinned at the way Belinda rolled her eyes. Belinda had disagreed with the use of the word 'epitome' from the start, claiming nobody would know what it meant. Bonnie, however, believed there was power in making the opposition feel ignorant.

Starre suddenly stood straighter as people glanced at one another. She obviously felt the same power that Bonnie did at their ignorance.

'However,' she said in her clear voice, 'for your sake we will also give the definition supplied by those who are misled by some people's frightening fantasies.'

Belinda's doubtful expression slowly transformed into a smile as Starre continued speaking. The voice which had begun so timidly was now filled with determination and conviction.

* * *

Starre and Bonnie caught up with Blaze as he headed toward the school gate that afternoon. Starre had completely recovered from her nerves and was now excited as she faced her brother.

'Guess what? We won.'

'I heard.' He smiled. 'Well done!'

'Well done?' Bonnie was confused. 'I thought you were totally against our case.'

'Totally against your arguments, not your team. That's what debating is about – supplying convincing arguments without getting personally involved. I disagree with your arguments but agree that you presented them very well.'

Bonnie fell silent. He was a good sport. She looked across at his serious expression and couldn't help pushing him further. 'So we were convincing?'

'Yes, but you were wrong.'

'You mean we did all that work and managed to be

convincing enough for the expert judges, but not for you?'

'That's right.'

'So nothing will ever change your mind?'

He looked at her. 'I hope and pray not. But some day, Bonnie, I pray with all my heart that I can convince you of what I believe. I wish I could explain it to the whole world; help them understand, but I'm really not good at explaining. I just upset people.'

Bonnie was saved from responding as a Year Seven student walked past.

'Hey, pimples!' His tone was mocking as he sneered at Blaze. 'Better pray over those two! They're probably possessed!'

Bonnie saw the way Starre tried to shrink out of view and Blaze blushed at the insult directed at him.

'Hey, get a horse!' Bonnie yelled back to the student, giving him such a condescending look he squirmed and moved on his way.

Starre chuckled and shook her head. 'Get a horse?'

Bonnie grinned. 'It was a bit ridiculous,' she admitted, 'but it was the first thing that came into my head.'

Blaze, however, was not smiling and all confidence and conviction had left his eyes.

'Don't let that kid's comment get to you.' Bonnie put an arm around his shoulder as Starre leapt onto her horse and headed home. Bonnie felt Blaze become tense at her touch and saw his cheeks grow a deeper shade of red.

'Hey, you're not shy of affection are you?' she asked with a laugh, wondering at his reaction. No one else had ever responded that way to her friendly, familiar touch. At his shrug, she moved closer with a playful grin. When he stepped away she took pity on him and stopped her teasing. She began her cheerful chatter all the way home.

Once home, Bonnie couldn't help thinking of Blaze's reaction to her touch. Her actions had never been considered romantic by the opposite sex. In some ways she was considered 'one of the boys'. From her first day of kindergarten when she punched Brad Jenson for taking her lunch, she had been respected and accepted by the boys and invited to take part in their active games. A tomboy in many ways, and yet so feminine in others, she was accepted by both genders as an equal and friend.

Bonnie smiled at the memory of Brad's bleeding nose, then realised Blaze Clements had no idea of her past. Could he be thinking her intentions were romantic? This in mind, she decided to go and pay him a visit and set him straight.

Her intentions were forgotten the moment she arrived at Collagg's Waterfall. The family sat around their unlit campfire, silent and despondent.

'Hey, why the gloom?'

Johnny's round face cheered up at the sight of her. 'They don't want to go to school anymore.' He splayed his large, grubby hands out in front of him in a helpless gesture. 'You're just what I need, Lady Lightning. You might be able to change their minds.'

She looked into each pair of eyes and saw the outright defiance in Storm and Beauty. Somehow she doubted she could influence them but she liked a challenge. It was worth a try.

'What's the problem with school?'

No one answered, but she thought she could guess. 'You know, I could help you fit in.'

Five pairs of eyes lifted enquiringly.

'I mean, that's if you want to.'

Storm's eyes snapped at her. 'I don't want to.'

Starre finally told her the problem. 'There's so many rules, and everyone's so proper at school, Bonnie. They're all so neat and tidy. Their uniforms look as if they've been ironed every day. They all think they're better than us.'

Bonnie tried to hide a smile. This family was certainly

not trained in cleanliness. And if anyone came across as being snobbish, it was Starre. Bonnie had heard several students accuse the circus girl of thinking she was a cut above everybody else. Her quiet, stand-offish ways had created an aversion to her which would not easily be reversed.

'I can help you,' Bonnie said, eyes sparkling, 'but I'd need to take you shopping.'

'So take me shopping, then.' Hope filled Misty's eyes.

'You got money?'

'Course I have. I've worked for years. No one works in the circus without getting paid.'

'What about you, Storm?' Bonnie ruffled his messy hair. 'Sure you don't want a haircut and some new clothes? Maybe a new school bag?'

'Certain,' he growled, 'Try Prince. He's the one who cares how he looks.'

'Prince?'

Prince grinned with the same playful, amused grin Misty had given. 'Yeah, I'll come along for the ride.'

Bonnie turned to Starre, Beauty and Blaze. 'How about you?'

They nodded, and watched as she turned to Johnny, her eyes questioning. He gave a delighted laugh. 'Come on now, Bonnie, I've got no reason to look for nice clothes. I don't have anyone to impress. My show days are over.'

'But don't you care about it for your own sake? You'll feel much better about the world if you know you look smart and tidy.'

'I'll feel much better about the world if I feel comfortable,' he assured her with another chuckle. 'I appreciate what you're doing for my kids, but don't bother with me, thanks.'

* * *

Bonnie was impressed by how quickly Prince and Starre

discovered their own style. They actually had quite good taste and it wasn't too different from that of others their age. At first Starre stood back as everyone else chose what they liked. Coming to her aid, Bonnie pointed out the colours that would match her olive skin and dark eyes. She was by far the most enchanting of them all and Bonnie found it thoroughly satisfying to enrich her poise and natural beauty through her clothing.

It was also Starre who agreed to buy an iron and iron all their school uniforms once she learned how to use it. The only problem would be finding space in their small caravans for an ironing board. Bonnie wondered at how quickly the girl's stand-offish manner disappeared to reveal a pleasant, intelligent nature.

Blaze, on the other hand, was a pain in the neck as he played her along. Bonnie got the distinct feeling he was getting her back for embarrassing him with talk about kissing and affection.

He screwed up his face at the modern, classy shirt Bonnie held up. 'What's so different about wearing a shirt like this and the shirts I have at home?'

'For a start, this is clean.'

He rolled his eyes and insisted dirt didn't bother him.

'Well, you're the only one it doesn't bother, so at least wear clean clothes for everyone else if you won't do it for yourself.' She saw the mischievous sparkle in his eyes and put her hands on her hips in a challenge. He shrugged and went to try the shirt on. He soon returned with Prince by his side and Bonnie stared in awe. Starre came over to inspect her brothers.

'Hey, you guys look good!'

'They do!' Beauty agreed, oblivious to her own improved appearance. 'Except your pimples clash with the colour of the shirt, Blaze.'

Prince gave his sister a dark look. 'Don't be such a cat, Beauty! Wait 'til you start coming out with them.'

She gave a harsh laugh and turned away. 'I've never had them before and I don't expect to get them.'

Bonnie was impressed with the way Blaze refused to react but found herself itching to retaliate on his behalf. Why would anyone want to hurt Blaze like that? He was actually very good looking despite those pimples. And even more so now he was wearing clean, smart clothes.

As they went to the checkout Misty let out a groan, 'I've lost my purse.'

'Again?' Starre began to look around. 'Did you leave it in the change rooms?'

'Good thinking!' Misty raced back and disappeared behind the heavy cream curtain. She returned a moment later, carrying her purse and wearing her wide, dimpled smile.

'Got it!' she called before tripping over the end of a clothes rack. Unfazed, she continued on her way to join them at the checkout. Bonnie watched in amazement as she opened her purse upside down and coins rolled across the floor.

Immediately, Blaze dropped to his knees and began collecting the coins. Bonnie joined him, trying not to chuckle at the situation. Spending a day with the Clements family was far from boring. Blaze picked up the final coin and took the ones Bonnie held out for him. He gave her a lopsided grin.

'Thanks for your help. Misty's our rough and reckless one. Always dropping things and losing things.' His voice was quiet and he was looking at Misty with tenderness. For a moment Bonnie wished he would look at her like that. She had noticed the way he looked at all his brothers and sisters. It was clear he cared for them deeply.

The shopping trip continued with no further mishaps but Bonnie was amazed at the amount they spent without blinking an eye. Money truly seemed to be no barrier. It was weariness rather than lack of finances that finally caused them to call it a day. Pleasantly tired and satisfied, they headed home with neat, modern haircuts and arms laden with clothes.

Chapter Four

Bonnie showed Starre how to use the iron, while Blaze watched with interest. They had needed to use an extension lead to set the ironing up outside the caravans.

'How can you stand living in something that doesn't even have room for an ironing board?' Bonnie wanted to know.

'Easily,' Blaze shrugged. 'They're bigger than you think.'

Bonnie snorted in disbelief. 'They're smaller than my bathroom at home!'

'You'd be surprised. Have a look.' He led her to his caravan and opened the door.

Bonnie let out a gasp. 'This is a pigsty!'

He merely grinned.

'No, seriously, how can you live like this?' She couldn't share his amusement as she looked from dirty clothes strewn across the floor to boots, hats, saddles and horse brushes piled up on the cupboards.

He shrugged. 'I've never lived any other way, but I'm not showing you the contents. I'm showing you the layout.'

'How can I see the layout, though?' Bonnie finally laughed. Blaze clearly had no idea how unusual his family's lifestyle was. 'It's hidden somewhere under all that stuff.'

Her eyes fell to the one tidy place in the van. Neatly stacked up were several large books. He followed her gaze. 'They're my theology books.'

'Theology?'

'Yeah. About life and God. It's hard to be a part of a church when you are travelling in the circus, so I've had to learn about God through the Bible and books about Him.'

She knew he was hoping she would ask more, but she could think of nothing to ask. 'I don't think I could stand to live in such a small space,' she finally told him. 'I'd feel too cramped.'

'Well, I've never lived in a house, so I don't know any different.'

She stared. 'Have you ever stayed in one?'

'I don't remember ever being in one.'

Bonnie couldn't believe her ears. She grabbed his hand. 'Come with me.'

'Where?'

'I want to show you my house and introduce you to my parents.'

He glanced at his clothes and Bonnie looked too. After a day of shopping his clothes weren't as dirty as usual, but he looked so insecure.

'Don't worry about how you look,' Bonnie reassured him. 'My parents won't judge you on that. They're pretty easy going.'

Bonnie was right. Her parents smiled at Blaze in a friendly manner. Bonnie was relieved to see Blaze relax despite the foreign environment.

'I'm pleased to finally meet you,' Mr Blake gave a warm pat on the back. 'I've heard a lot about you.'

'You have? Should I be worried?'

Bonnie grinned as she plonked herself on the lounge chair beside him. 'Come on, Blaze. Why should you be worried? I only told them about your rugged good looks and tendency to be too serious.'

'Too serious?'

'Yes. If you weren't so serious, you'd know I'm only joking about your seriosity.'

'Seriosity? What kind of word is that?' Blaze chuckled before returning his attention to Mr Blake. 'Has she always been this cheerful and carefree?'

Mr Blake smiled an affectionate smile in her direction. 'Yeah … I guess she has.'

* * *

'You have a nice family,' Blaze said quietly as Bonnie walked him home.

She had to agree. 'Yeah, I do. I'm blessed that way.'

'Blessed? You think someone's blessed you?'

She shrugged. 'I guess I meant lucky.'

'Oh.' He looked disappointed and she studied him.

'You think God gave me my family, don't you?'

'Yeah. I mean, if you're blessed, someone has to have blessed you, don't they?'

'I s'pose. I haven't really thought about it much before.'

'But if someone has given you all these good things in life, don't you want to know who it is so that you can thank them?'

'Not really. Things are pretty good as they are and I'm not going to bother disturbing them.'

He kicked at a stone. His voice was strained as he stopped and looked deep into her eyes. 'I wonder if that's why you haven't recognised the need for God in your life. You've got a relaxed, loving, family environment, a naturally happy nature … you've got it pretty good, really. With a dad like that it's no wonder you don't long for your Heavenly Father. I envy you in some way but in the ways that count—'

'Come on, Blaze.' Bonnie cut him off and nudged his foot with the toe of her running shoe. 'How could you ever envy me? Growing up in a circus with all those horses is something I could only dream of … Hey, can I ride one of your horses? I mean, on my own?'

It was an obvious attempt to change the subject, but Blaze let it be.

'Which one?'

'The biggest and fastest.'

'That would be Victorian Dream. She can be a bit restless, though. You might want to start with Penny Drop.'

'That little pony thing?' Bonnie was incredulous. 'You've got to be kidding!'

'She's less likely to throw you off.'

'Blaze, I don't want to meander around. I want to ride!'

Blaze shook his head, but she sensed he was about to give in. His smile told her the exact moment when he did. The shake of his head also told her he was frustrated with himself.

'Aren't you afraid of anything?'

She chuckled. 'No, and I can tell you it's a great way to live.'

'Don't you worry about getting hurt; the normal things most people are scared of?'

'I've never thought about it. Why worry about things that might not even happen?'

He sighed. 'Look Bonnie, I know I might lose your friendship here, but I care enough to ask …' He swallowed hard. 'What about death? Everyone dies. Aren't you scared of dying?'

'No. Even if you're right about there being a heaven, I expect God will let me in.'

Blaze shuffled uncomfortably. 'You're saying you've never done anything wrong?'

Bonnie laughed. 'I wouldn't dare suggest that,' she admitted, 'but I've never broken any of the Ten Commandments or anything.'

'Which ones haven't you broken?'

She shrugged, wondering what he was getting at. 'All of them, I guess. I've never stolen or murdered or ...' she tried to remember what the commandments were.

'You've never used God's name as a swear word?' he pressed. 'Or lied, or said something disrespectful to your parents or thought badly of them?'

She stared at him, saying nothing but knowing she was at a disadvantage when it came to arguments on the Bible.

'Have you ever put anything first in your life apart from God?' His look turned gentle when she stared at him blankly. 'That's the first commandment.'

Bonnie snorted. 'If that's the requirement to get into heaven, no one can get in!'

'True. That's why Jesus died in our place. If we give Him our lives, He becomes our representative.'

Bonnie crossed her arms and raised her chin, feeling angry and defensive for the first time.

'You're suggesting God would send me to hell, aren't you?' Her eyes bored into his. 'I don't believe a God of love would do that without giving people a fair chance.'

'Perhaps this is your chance.' Blaze looked away and began kicking a stone in his path. She felt irritated. Couldn't he at least have the courage to look at her while he so blatantly challenged her? She was beginning to wonder why she ever liked this guy in the first place.

'My chance? Why do I need a chance when I don't even believe God exists?'

He kicked the stone again. 'Not believing doesn't mean it's

not true.' He kept his head down, refusing to meet her piercing gaze. 'God never forces us to do anything. He gives us a choice. We can choose to live for Him or live for ourselves –'

Bonnie didn't wait for him to finish. She spun on her heel and headed back home without another word. If Blaze was going to start preaching at her, she would have nothing more to do with him!

As Bonnie lay in bed that night, her mind tumbled over. Blaze was so serious and arrogant; so proud to force his beliefs onto her! Yet at the same time, something drew her to him. Maybe it was his good looks. It only took her a few moments to laugh at her ridiculous conclusion. If it were looks she was after, Prince was the attractive one. Blaze's pimples denied him the privilege of being considered handsome. She punched her pillow in frustration.

'I was content with life until the Clements family arrived but now something isn't right.'

She was tempted to avoid them altogether, but that would prove quite difficult with them living in the paddock next door and going to the same school. Besides, Bonnie usually liked to face challenges head on, and avoiding the Clements family wasn't going to sort anything out.

As she lay awake, Bonnie felt an emptiness she had never felt before. Time and time again she attempted to push away the memory of Blaze's words and the earnest dark eyes imploring her to understand.

Chapter Five

'Blaze, wait!' Bonnie could see Blaze heading toward the school gate to go home and she desperately wanted to talk to him. He turned, and to her relief, waited. His expression said he wasn't angry with her. She caught her breath as she reached him.

'You riding home with one of the others?'

'You didn't have to run,' His smile was warm and the challenging tone of yesterday had disappeared, 'and no, I'm not riding.'

They walked side by side for a while, Bonnie's mind running over yesterday's conversation. If he wasn't going to mention it, neither was she. She needed to direct the conversation as far away from the topic as possible. Something that interested both of them but wouldn't cause disagreement. Horses. That was it.

'Why don't you buy yourself another horse? Then you wouldn't have to walk home every day. It's not like you don't have enough money.'

He smiled at her blunt reminder of his financial situation. 'Perhaps one day.'

'Why not now?'

He hesitated, then met her eyes with an honest, frank look. 'I don't want to become obsessed with horses again.' He began to say something, then stopped and spoke carefully. 'There are much more important things in life than horses! Anyway, not having a horse gives me opportunities I wouldn't otherwise have.'

'Such as?'

He shuffled and avoided her eyes. 'Well, it gives me an opportunity to get to know people more.'

'Like me?' A delighted chuckle escaped her.

'Well ...'

Her grin was wide as she gave him a friendly poke. 'Come on. You like me, don't you?'

The colour of his cheeks deepened noticeably. 'Not in the way you're meaning.'

She wondered what compelled her to tease him so much. It so clearly bothered him and he made such an effort to have it all together. Maybe that's why she so enjoyed taking him off guard. She decided to give him space.

'What will you name your new horse?'

He gave her a sideways look and she could tell he was amused.

'I haven't said I'm getting one.'

'I'd name it Peter Pan.'

'Peter Pan? Why?'

'Because being on a horse is as good as flying. Racing against the wind makes me feel like I'm living forever. Like I'll never grow old ... Blaze? What's wrong?'

He had hung his head and his eyes were filled with anguish.

'Come on, Blaze. Tell me.'

He raised his head slowly and she drew in a deep breath. Somehow she had hurt him. Deeply.

'I just wish, I wish you would believe and really live forever.'

'What?'

He kicked a stone along the road in a manner she was becoming familiar with, then took a deep breath. 'Bonnie, I can't help sharing my beliefs with you. They're too much a part of who I am. But at the same time, I don't want to say the wrong thing and lose your friendship. Still, I'd prefer to risk making you my enemy than never give you a chance to be my friend forever in heaven.'

When she said nothing, he stopped. She stopped too.

'Why are you so focused on me? So many people don't believe in God. I'm not the only one.'

'I care about you.'

'Why?' Her tone wasn't accusatory, just curious.

'Because you're lost. Spiritually, you're lost.'

'I'm content with my life.'

'But surely if you're honest with yourself you would worry about death? You know it's inevitable.'

'No. I'm alive right now. I live for the moment, Blaze.' With that, she gave him a playful grin and began walking again. 'If only you would live for the moment, too. We could really have something going, you and I! You have to admit there's a bit of a spark between us.'

His look was a mixture of shock and confusion. Colour once again crept into his cheeks. 'Don't tease, Bonnie.'

She stopped ahead of him, surprised that he hadn't fallen into step beside her.

'Come on, Blaze! Don't be so serious all the time. We weren't born to worry.'

He came to her like a magnet, his look intense. She could get lost in those eyes if she wasn't careful.

'What were we born for then, Bonnie? What do you believe you were born for?'

It was a new thought for her. 'I don't really know, I guess. For life – for the now?'

'What about the future?'

'I'll worry about that when it comes.'

Blaze gave a resigned sigh. 'I can see this conversation is getting nowhere.'

'You're right there. Let's talk about something more cheerful.'

She grinned at him and to her relief, he allowed her to begin her lighthearted, everyday chatter. Yet she knew he still looked at her with concern. If only she could get through to him he really didn't need to worry about her spiritual well-being.

* * *

Bonnie sat at the kitchen table preparing a debate for the beginning of the new season, but it was hard to concentrate. She kept thinking of things Blaze had said or done. With a sigh, she struggled to focus. Why did he capture so many of her thoughts? In some ways he and his ideas were like an annoying fly she couldn't shoo away. But then, she found herself seeking out his company. What was that about? She had told her father about his strange way of thinking and he agreed the circus boy was messed up somewhere.

'I'm surprised you've made friends with someone like Blaze Clements.'

Bonnie looked up quickly. Her father was now pouring himself a glass of water and she couldn't read his expression.

'Don't get me wrong, it's not that I disapprove of your friendship. I like the lad.' He gave her a sideways grin, 'Show boy ways and all. It's just that he's so religious.'

'He is.' Bonnie leaned back in her chair. 'And that's why we can never be more than friends.'

Her father raised his brows. 'You'd like to be more than friends?'

Bonnie giggled, tapping the pen she held against her chin. 'Come on, Dad. You know I've got no time for romance.'

'Really?' He looked at her over his glasses. 'It's got to happen sometime, Bonnie. You're not a little girl anymore.'

Bonnie suddenly felt uncomfortable and shuffled her notes around. Her father gave a teasing grin.

'You have to admit he's a good looking lad apart from the pimples.'

Bonnie nodded. 'He has a thing about those pimples. I don't know why he's so worried about them. I think the kids at school only tease him because he reacts so much when they pick on him.'

Her father nodded as he came and took the chair beside hers. 'Quite likely. Your Uncle Bill says he gets along well with most students, though.'

'Uncle Bill? Have you been checking out Blaze's credentials?' Bonnie laughed and threw a pen at her father. 'Don't you trust my friends?'

He grinned and tossed the pen back to her. 'Of course I trust your friends. It's you I don't trust. I had to check how many times you've been sent out of class lately, and Uncle Bill just happened to mention that Blaze works with you in the art room most weeks.'

Bonnie smiled. She definitely didn't mind being sent to the deputy head for misbehaving in Miss Sander's class. Not only did it mean she could enjoy being in a more interesting class conducted by her Uncle; it also meant she would be met by Blaze's amused look as he moved over to give her space beside him. Her artistic skills were developing so much faster than anyone else in her class. However, for the first time in her life she was falling behind in Geography.

The very next day Blaze challenged her with, 'I really would have thought you'd grow out of this.' Despite his gruff tone, amusement remained in his dark eyes.

Bonnie raised her chin and gave him a defiant look. 'If Miss Sanders was a more interesting teacher I wouldn't become so restless and distracting.'

'Never your fault; always someone else's, hey? Little Miss Perfect.'

She flipped a ruler at him in response and prepared her paints. 'Stop talking. I don't want to sit here discussing the behaviour of some delinquent student. I have work to do.'

With a grin that matched hers, he obliged. As she worked, Bonnie wondered at his comment. He had been teasing, but did she really always put the blame on other people and avoid facing that she, Bonnie Blake, might have weaknesses? It was an annoying thought that would not go away.

Chapter Six

The more time Bonnie spent with Blaze, the more she was attracted to him.

'I think it's his eyes that get to me,' she confided in her mother as she helped prepare the evening meal. 'Half the time he annoys me with the things he says, but all he has to do is look at me out of those big, dark eyes and I can't help forgiving him. If he'd just stop talking about God all the time.'

Mrs Blake took one of the potatoes Bonnie had peeled and began to dice it. 'You know, your father and I have different religious beliefs. I always went to church as a child and I believe in God. Perhaps not quite the way Blaze does. I mean, I believe he's up there …'

Bonnie's eyes widened in surprise. Her mother was confessing to faith in a God she had never even mentioned before. Curious, she leaned back on the bench to study her mother.

'Isn't that what Blaze believes?'

'I think he takes it more seriously. I've come across people like that before. They believe God talks to them and that they are personal friends with Him or something.'

Bonnie couldn't remember Blaze admitting to anything like that, neither had she ever asked him exactly what he did believe.

'So what does Dad believe?'

'I'm not totally sure. He never went to church or anything, and doesn't believe in God. I think he believes in evolution.'

'Evolution?'

'He believes Charles Darwin's theory; that the world evolved over millions of years.'

Bonnie stared at her mother in wonder, her thoughts racing fast. Her parents had beliefs about religion and how the world came into being? Why did they need to believe anything? Beliefs about the world and life only seemed to complicate things and distract from the enjoyment of living. It was a hopeless case anyway. Everyone had their opinions, so how could anyone claim to know the truth? And yet, if there really was truth out there, Bonnie felt a desperate longing to find it. There was no time to waste and she raced out the door. She had to speak with Blaze.

Her curiosity over how someone could believe God spoke to them was beginning to drive her crazy. It was too ridiculous to be true. Blaze was different, but he didn't strike her as being that weird. He'd never talked about hearing voices or seeing things. Surely he didn't believe that God Himself was his friend?

To her disappointment, Misty was the only one sitting in the 'lounge room' as they called the logs placed like seats around the campfire. Misty's eyes lit up at the sight of Bonnie. 'How are you?' She stood up and offered a seat, then held out the cracked glass in her hand. 'Want a drink?'

Bonnie wasn't certain that Misty hadn't already drunk from the dirty glass, and so politely declined. 'No thanks, you have it.' She watched to see if the water would make it to the circus girl's dimpled mouth without being spilled. It didn't.

'So, you're here to see Blaze?' Misty brushed at the wet patch on her shirt and gave Bonnie her bright, friendly smile.

'Yeah. Is he here?'

'Everyone's just down at the creek having a swim. I don't think they'll be long.'

'You're not swimming?'

'No. I ripped my swimmers on an old log yesterday. I haven't fixed 'em yet.'

Bonnie smiled. How could someone so careful and nimble in some ways, and be so clumsy and careless in others?

'He's worried about you.' Misty took another sip from the cracked glass. 'He really wants you to believe in his God.'

'Yeah, I know, it's a bit of a pain. He really doesn't need to worry about me. '

An indefinable expression passed over Misty's face. Bonnie was about to question her when voices were heard coming up over the rise. The afternoon swim was over.

'G'day Lady Lightning! Come to see us?' Johnny bellowed with surprised pleasure. He held out a large hand for Bonnie to shake. Gingerly she did, trying to ignore his dirty fingernails.

'Actually, just Blaze.' Bonnie turned to smile in Blaze's direction. He was putting on his boots and looked surprised that she had sought him out.

He finished doing up his boot then came to her. 'What's up?'

'Just wanted to talk.' She glanced around at the Clements family who were all watching her with interest. She lowered her voice. 'Can we go for a walk or something?'

She hadn't intended for anyone else to hear, but they did and Johnny let out a loud laugh and whistle while Prince smiled knowingly toward Starre. Blaze shook his head at them. His face turned slightly red. He took Bonnie's hand. 'We'll be back later.'

Surprised by his actions and deeply aware of the warmth of his hand around hers, Bonnie tried to think sensibly. Blaze had always avoided touch. Until now. Her mother's words turned over in her mind. 'Your father and I have different beliefs ...'

Blaze seemed to realise his hand had captured her own and he gently released it, looking anywhere but directly at her.

'So what's up?' His voice had come out deep and gruff and she knew he was attempting to disguise his discomfort. She waited until he finally looked at her, and smiled warmly into his eyes.

'I just have some questions about what you believe and stuff.'

She felt, rather than heard his gasp as he stopped in his tracks and faced her, looking rather dazed. 'What?'

He swallowed hard. 'I just never thought this would really happen. I mean I prayed it would and I tried not to preach or bring up my beliefs too much in case I scared you away … and here you are, asking me straight out what I believe.'

Bonnie laughed. 'Blaze, if I knew it meant so much to you, I could have thought of questions to ask!'

'It's not just that.' His voice turned husky. 'It's the fact that God answered my prayer. I mean I know he answers prayer, but I didn't know if He could work in people's lives when they don't even believe in him. Do you know what I mean?'

'I think so, but it's coincidence, Blaze. I mean, you talk about it all the time, so of course I have questions.'

He shook his head. 'No, this isn't coincidence.' He began walking again, new confidence in his stride. 'So, what are your questions?'

Blaze had just answered one of them. It seemed he truly did talk to God and believe God answered. But not in a weird way. He was just talking about prayer.

'You said you pray for me.'

'Every day.'

'Seriously? Every day?'

'Sometimes many times throughout the day.'

'Why?' She was aware she sounded blunt, but he had caught her by surprise with his admission.

'Because I care.'

'But what do you pray?'

At that question, he fell silent and seemed to weigh up his words. Finally his eyes met hers. She couldn't help noticing how attractive his dark eyes and sun-browned face were, pimples or no pimples.

'I pray that you will come to know God.'

'Know God?' She screwed up her nose, acutely aware that all her questions were being answered before she had a chance to ask. 'What kind of a concept is that?'

'Not a concept. A reality. We were born to have a relationship with God.'

'But you can't even see Him. How can you know Him?'

Blaze's brow furrowed and he took his time answering. 'It's hard to explain to someone who doesn't even believe.'

'Can you try?'

He thought a few moments more. 'Well, I find out what God's like by reading the Bible. It tells me what Jesus was like when He was on earth, and Jesus was God in human form.' He frowned slightly. 'And I know you'll think this is a bit out there, but it's like I have this voice – no, not exactly a voice – kind of a knowing in my heart when he's telling me something.'

He was right. It did sound a bit 'out there'. In fact, the whole thing seemed highly questionable.

'Well I've got plenty of friends.' Bonnie shrugged. 'I don't need the worry of building a relationship with someone I can't even see or hear.'

When he didn't respond, she knew her attitude had caused him grief once again.

'What will it take for you to believe, Bonnie?'

She shrugged again. 'Keep praying. God might just answer that prayer, too!'

'I'll always hope.' He spoke so quietly she almost missed it.

Chapter Seven

School was out for the day and Bonnie was sprinting across the paddocks. The athletics carnival was only a few days away and she desperately wanted to take a few seconds off her time. She heard the familiar pounding of horses' hooves behind her and turned to see Beauty approaching on Montford Express.

'Bonnie, have you seen Starre?' Beauty's eyes were wide with something close to terror. Bonnie slowed to a jog, trying to catch her breath. She came to a complete stop while Beauty dismounted.

'No. Didn't she go home from school with you?' Bonnie bent over, taking in big gulps of air.

'She went to get a couple of things from the shops first and we haven't seen her since.'

Bonnie straightened and looked at her watch. That was at least two hours ago. The athletics carnival meant a lot to her, but training would have to finish for this afternoon – it seemed that Starre Clements might be in trouble.

Bonnie knew Beauty's condescending attitude too well but hoped she wouldn't need to suffer it now. 'I'll help you look. Can I fit on your horse?'

Beauty helped her up. There was no time for animosity.

'Let's try the shopping Centre in Broden Street first,' Bonnie suggested as the horse broke into a canter.

The search in Broden Street only succeeded in finding Prince coming out of Heather's Underwear Boutique holding Kylie Sandom's hand. His cheeks flushed as he noticed them.

Beauty was clearly incensed. 'What do you think you're doing, Prince? You're supposed to be helping us look for Starre but you're here spending all your money on underwear for some girl you'll be sick of in a week. Starre's our sister.'

Kylie glared as she moved threateningly toward Beauty. 'You little cat.'

Bonnie stepped between them. 'Prince, please, don't you think you could help us find Starre?'

Prince's expression darkened to match Beauty's. His eyes snapped. 'No. Starre is probably doing what I'm doing and trying to find a bit of space.' His voice softened at Bonnie's stunned look. 'Sorry, I know it's not your fault I need a break, but I'm sure Starre feels like me and just wants to enjoy being an individual every now and then.' He shook his head wearily. 'We're not glued together just because we're triplets, you know.'

Beauty looked devastated. Then she stood straighter and opened her mouth, clearly about to tell Prince exactly what he could do with his individuality. Sensing a scene about to develop, Bonnie grabbed Beauty's arm.

'Let's keep looking.'

And so they rushed around the centre.

'Have you seen my sister?' Beauty asked every person who looked as though they might not be in a hurry. Then Beauty suddenly looked as though she'd seen a ghost.

'Montford! I've left Montford out there on the street. Marcos could find him!'

Starre was forgotten as Beauty raced from the centre,

seeming to forget that Bonnie had no way of getting home. Bonnie shook her head in bewilderment, stunned at the attitude of both Prince and Beauty. Their sister was missing and all they could think of was themselves or their precious horses!

'Hey, Bonnie!'

Bonnie turned to see Blaze coming toward her from the entrance of the centre. His expression told her nothing. 'We've found her.'

'She's okay?'

'I don't know. Dad's gone to get her.'

Bonnie gazed at him, waiting for an explanation. Nothing was making sense.

'The circus is heading this way and Marcos reckons she rode back there this afternoon and asked for work.' Blaze's dark eyes clouded with strain, revealing how worried he really was. 'Which is crazy, since they threatened to kidnap her a few months ago. Johnny's not too worried about the whole thing, but I'm not going to let her get off that lightly!'

Bonnie listened to the anger in his tone. This was a forceful, determined Blaze Clements she hadn't seen before. Yet the anger was clearly springing from a deep concern for his sister.

She rested her hand lightly on his shoulder, trying to calm him down. 'Has she really done anything wrong?'

'Definitely. Going back is the most dangerous thing she could do! Marcos wants our horses more than anything.'

'But obviously Starre wants to be back there, too.'

Blaze looked defeated for a moment. He sat down on the seat outside the store, and Bonnie sat beside him. She felt the sigh that came from somewhere deep inside him.

'Starre hasn't been the same since we left, Bonnie. She's a different person. In the circus she was the outgoing one; always crazy and having fun. Sometimes she'd have us laughing so hard we couldn't get anything done. It used to annoy Marcos 'cause we'd get so behind in our performance practice, but she could even get him laughing sometimes. Now everyone sees her as a snob, when really, well, Beauty is the real snob!'

Bonnie listened in surprise. Starre outgoing and carefree? Starre sure must have changed since she left the circus. Maybe she did miss it enough that she would risk everything to go back.

'So your Dad's not worried about the possibility of Starre being kidnapped?'

'Johnny isn't worried about anything.'

'Not even his own daughter?'

'I don't know. I just don't know anything right now.' The creases returned to Blaze's forehead as he took Bonnie's arm. 'Let's go home.'

Prince hadn't arrived home, but a tearful Misty was sitting beside an unimpressed Storm and Beauty

'Come on, Misty!' Storm snapped when Misty burst into tears at the sight of Blaze and Bonnie. 'Crying isn't going to do anything.'

Blaze just put comforting arms around his sister and looked to Storm, his voice tight and strained. 'Heard anything yet?'

'No, apart from Misty's sniffles. Can't you get a tissue, girl?'

'Go and get some sympathy from somewhere, Storm,' Blaze snapped at his brother, and had the situation not been so concerning, Bonnie would have smiled. Blaze was sounding more like herself by the day. In fact, he was very quickly conforming to everyday Aussie language and lifestyle outside the circus and Bonnie found that the more he changed, the more she liked him.

* * *

It was dark by the time Johnny arrived home with a subdued Starre in tow. By then, Bonnie had called her parents. They had arrived not much later with sandwiches for everyone. Their calm, confident nature made the situation seem a lot easier to handle.

Johnny swaggered over to the campfire, beaming. 'Well, here we are, and everything's fine.' He stopped when he saw Bonnie's parents and his smile disappeared. 'Mr and Mrs Blake! What a surprise. Well, everything's okay.' He waved his hand dismissively. 'Thanks for coming … although you didn't need to.'

Johnny was beaming again as though it had all been unnecessary drama. Bonnie was watching Blaze's expression. At his father's words he seemed to snap.

'They did need to come, Johnny!' His eyes were unusually cold, his voice tight. 'We needed some parental concern and support around here.'

Johnny looked shocked and his beaming smile almost faded for a moment, then his hesitation diminished as he grinned at Blaze impishly.

'Parental support? Your brothers and sisters have you, Blaze!'

'I know, Johnny, but I shouldn't need to be a father to my own brothers and sisters. If you did the job, I wouldn't need to!'

A look came to Johnny's face that said he felt like a hurt child. Misty, who was worn out by the long day, burst into tears again. Bonnie's father took over.

'I think some sleep will do everyone good. How about you leave all discussion until the morning?' The commanding tone in his voice was exactly what everyone needed when everything seemed so out of control. One by one the family headed to bed, Storm disappearing first.

'Are you okay?' Bonnie managed to whisper to Starre before she retired. Starre turned desperate, pleading eyes to meet hers.

'Bonnie, I need your help! Tomorrow we have to talk!'

Bonnie only had time to nod before Starre disappeared

into the van she shared with her sisters. With nothing more to do, the tired Blake family headed home. Bonnie couldn't help remembering with amazement the scene that had unfolded before them. Certainly, the Clements family was not like any other she had come across. But no longer was Bonnie fascinated. Instead, she was deeply concerned.

'No wonder Blaze turned to religion! If I had problems like that, I would call out to God for help, too!'

Chapter Eight

Bonnie awoke early and felt a desperate need to talk to Starre. Something wasn't right. Throwing on her clothes, she crept out of the house and began the walk through the back paddock and over the fence. She was just about to cross the small creek between their properties when she stopped. A lonely figure sat hunched on a rock beside the flowing water.

'Starre?'

Starre looked up and at the same moment, Blaze came over the top of the hill on the other side. Dark rings showed beneath his eyes and his jaw was set tight. His gaze swept the landscape then fell on Starre. He didn't even acknowledge Bonnie as he stalked toward his sister. 'What happened, Starre? What did you think you were doing?'

Starre stared up at her brother with wide, unrevealing eyes.

'Don't you care about what could have happened to everyone else?' Blaze's voice was rising in anger and Bonnie saw the way Starre's expression closed up. Blaze was going about this the wrong way and if he kept going, there was no way Starre would reveal anything.

'You might be grieving for the circus, but how could you be so selfish?' He swore and Starre cringed.

'Blaze, you don't swear anymore! Not since you gave your life to Jesus.'

Blaze softened, but only slightly. 'I haven't had reason to, until now.'

Starre rose on unsteady legs.

'How could you believe what Marcos says? You know he's a liar.'

She ran a weary hand across her face. 'Do you really think that after what you did for me, selling Elle Ripple, that I would be so ungrateful?' Her voice broke and she rushed away.

Blaze and Bonnie watched as Starre disappeared over the hill. Blaze looked stunned as the anger drained from his expression.'What's going on?'

Bonnie rested a hand on his arm. 'I think she's saying she didn't go to the circus of her own free will.'

Blaze shook his head. 'But she couldn't have been kidnapped – Marcos let Johnny bring her home without a fight. So what on earth is going on?'

Bonnie shrugged. 'I don't know, but I think we should try to find out. A bit more gently.'

Blaze looked up quickly and then smiled ruefully. 'Point taken. I think I know where she is.'

Bonnie followed Blaze further up the creek. Then he stopped and she followed his gaze to where Starre sat beneath an old hollowed out gum tree. He didn't approach her for a moment, but stood completely still, his eyes sliding shut. Bonnie guessed he was praying. Then, taking a deep breath, he moved toward Starre and squatted beside her. 'Starre, I'm sorry.'

She looked at him and tears glistened on her cheeks. 'I know you are. You were worried.'

Blaze settled himself at her side and dangled a hand in the cool water. His manner was now gentle and apologetic. 'I'm ready to listen.'

She remained silent for several minutes and then raised frightened eyes to his. 'Blaze, I can't tell you, but I promise I will tell someone.' She glanced to Bonnie, a message in her eyes. Bonnie knew she would be that someone as soon as Blaze left. If only Blaze would accept that. To her surprise, he did. He squeezed Starre's shoulder gently as he stood.

'I want to force you to tell me everything, but I know God's in control. Just make sure you do tell someone.'

With that he turned and made his way back to the caravans. Bonnie and Starre looked at one another for a long moment before Bonnie approached and took Blaze's seat.

Starre was crying, now. 'I couldn't tell him. I can't let him put his life on the line for me. He would, you know.'

Bonnie thought of the way Blaze looked out for his siblings; of his loving, protective streak. 'I know.'

Starre swiped at tears with the back of her hand. 'Clive and Banksie took me. They're from the circus. They took me in their truck – with Steadfast Ever. They want another horse and they threatened to put Steadfast down if I don't agree to get my family to sign contracts.' She took a deep breath and slowed down. 'They're just going to demand them all, one by one. I know it!'

Bonnie's mind was in a whirl. Starre was speaking about people and names she didn't recognise. She tried to remember who owned which horse. 'Steadfast Ever is your horse?'

'Yes.'

'And what are the contracts about?'

'To say we have left the horses as property of the circus.'

Bonnie frowned. This was serious.

'When Johnny got there to pick me up, they acted as if they had been trying to make me go home for hours. It made me sick!'

Bonnie felt sick too, as her mind began to conjure up all kinds of scenarios. 'Did they hurt you?'

'No, but they threatened to. Bonnie, they said if they can't have the horses, they want one of us to go back to the circus and train the horses they already have. That's why I couldn't tell Blaze. I don't want Blaze to go back to the circus.'

'Do you think he would?' Fear clutched at Bonnie's heart even as she knew the answer. Blaze loved his family so deeply. He had made himself their guardian, and he knew more than she did what those circus men were capable of.

'Blaze would do anything to save one of us or our horses,' Starre said, voicing Bonnie's exact thoughts. 'I mean, he gave up Elle Ripple last time.'

Bonnie fell silent in thought, while Starre shivered. It must be awful having the place and people she had once so loved turning into a nightmare. Bonnie wished she had some answers for Starre. For the first time in her life she wished there were a higher wisdom she could turn to. It would be nice to be able to turn to God and leave it all with Him right now.

Starre seemed resigned. 'Whatever way you look at it, Marcos has got us.' She waved a hand helplessly in the air. 'There's nothing I can do but play along with him. Blaze sold Elle Ripple to save my life, so I have to be willing to give up Steadfast, too. They still have him, anyway. I just wish Johnny had brought the horse float when he came to get me.'

'No, Starre!' Bonnie was not willing to give in that easily. 'There has to be a way out. You have to go to the police!'

'The police won't help.' Starre's shoulders slumped in defeat. 'Police don't get involved with the lives of circus people.'

Bonnie decided what to do.

* * *

The police station seemed eerily quiet when Bonnie entered. No one sat at the front desk, and even though the door buzzed repeatedly as she came through, no one came rushing to the front. The place seemed completely empty.

'Lucky I'm not an emergency!' Bonnie muttered, surprised by her own black thoughts. The Clements family certainly was upsetting her bright, easy-going world.

'G'day.' A smiling officer greeted her as he wandered in from the back room.

'Hello. Um, I want to report a crime.'

The officer's look was quizzical as he leant back in his chair. Definitely slouching, Bonnie thought.

'You're the Blake girl, aren't you?'

He was way too casual for Bonnie's liking. 'Yes, but it's not about me.'

'You witnessed the crime, though?'

'Not exactly.'

'Well, I don't know what you're expecting me to do.'

Anger filled Bonnie and she leaned over the desk. 'I expect you to take out your notebook and write down what I'm about to tell you. Whether or not I witnessed the crime doesn't change the fact that it occurred!'

The officer's eyes showed a hint of amusement as he slowly reached for his notebook.

'Conscientious little thing, aren't you?' He sat up straighter, pen poised. 'Fire away. I've got it covered.'

Bonnie felt humiliated by the way he so obviously humoured her, but there was nothing she could do about it. Every now and then he made a squiggle in his note book. Finally he stood and stretched.

'Your friend really needs to see me herself. I have all this recorded so if anything happens it's here, but until something happens, my hands are tied.'

'But you could do something if Starre came in?'

'Starre or one of the members of her family. Unless they want to charge these circus clowns, we can't lay a hand on them.'

Bonnie didn't miss his pun about circus clowns, and it frustrated her. This infuriating police officer simply wouldn't take her seriously! She left, deciding that the first thing she needed to do was convince Starre to report the threat to the police. However, after the performance of the policeman that afternoon, Bonnie understood why Starre wasn't convinced the law would be of any help.

Chapter Nine

Bonnie walked down to the chook pen to collect the eggs, deep in thought. Absently shooing a hen out of the nesting box, she remembered back to what Starre had told her about Marcos. How could she convince Starre to report this incident to the police? Copper began to bark, running wildly up and down the fence, and Bonnie looked up to see Blaze heading her way. His face was creased with worry as he strode toward her. Had Starre told him what had happened?

'What's up?' Bonnie attempted to smile at him, stepping over some horse manure.

Blaze studied her intently and she wondered how much he really did know. 'I needed some more pleasant company.'

'I can imagine. Is there still a volcano about to erupt in the Clements' Camp?'

Blaze shook his head grimly. 'It already has. We've had drama after drama lately.'

Bonnie frowned, unable to mask her concern. Surely Starre hadn't told Blaze the full story? She couldn't stand the thought of Blaze returning to the circus. 'What else has happened?'

'When Starre went back to the circus she discovered Prince has a daughter ... and Prince couldn't care less!' The darkness of his eyes revealed the depth of his anger and frustration over the news.

'Prince has a daughter?' Bonnie tried to imagine Prince being old enough to have a child. This was not the news she had expected to hear.

'Yeah. Prince is a real circus boy. I guess he hasn't ever known any other way of life and something about him attracts the girls. Johnny didn't really seem to care what we did and Prince was always going off and … well, you know.'

Bonnie was astounded. She had known the Clements family were unusual, but the more she found out the more disturbed she felt.

'Who … where is the … the partner?'

'It's Carrie, the daughter of the elephant trainer. Prince has had something going with her for years – only now, Prince won't admit it. He just can't accept responsibility.'

Blaze sighed and the concern in his expression tore at Bonnie's heart.

'Does Carrie want Prince to take responsibility for the baby?'

'I don't know, but he should. This is my niece we're talking about. Sky, her name is. I hate to think that any relative of mine is not being properly cared for and being brought up in that circus!'

Bonnie studied Blaze silently. He was full of compassion for a niece he had never even met. What was it about Blaze that made him so concerned for other people? Sometimes he seemed old beyond his years. Prince, on the other hand, seemed childish in comparison. How ironic that Prince was the father!

'I wish she was my daughter!' Blaze stopped, realising what he'd just said. 'I don't mean I wish I'd done something so irresponsible and immoral. I just wish I had the authority to take her and care for her. But there's no way we can ever go back to the circus now.'

Bonnie's mind tumbled over as she tried to imagine Blaze Clements in a circus scene where immature teenagers became parents. But she wondered then if the circus was really so different from the outside world. She knew several of the teenage girls in Everdeen had become pregnant and then had abortions. As Bonnie studied Blaze she knew he would be even more horrified at the thought of abortion. Blaze valued life and people and she could only put his compassion down to his faith in God.

'Were you ever a circus boy with circus values like Prince? I mean, before you started believing in God?'

Blaze shook his dark head. 'No. I guess my pimples have been a blessing in some ways.'

'What do you mean?'

'I mean I hate the way I look, but it protected me from …' he blushed uncomfortably, 'well, from having girls interested in me.'

'You don't like the way you look?'

'Well, I can't say pimples are very attractive.' Blaze's voice was gruff. 'If I want to get married some day they could be a problem.'

Bonnie stared, dumbfounded. Then she found her tongue. 'I don't think you'll remain a bachelor all your life just because you've got a few pimples. Anyway, they'll probably go when you're older.'

'Maybe, but for now—' He stopped short as Bonnie's eyes sparkled with mischief.

She took a step closer and waved a hand toward his face. 'So you've got a few pimples? Deal with them!'

Blaze gave her a cautious look. 'Bonnie …'

His warning tone had the opposite effect on Bonnie and she grinned, unable to help provoking.

'I would have you if you didn't care so much that I don't

follow your religion. I know, I know, not religion … your God. Whatever. It's all the same to me. Anyway, don't you believe your God created you? Do you think He made a mistake?'

Blaze shook his head as he backed away to put space between them. 'When will you stop stirring and take me seriously?'

'When you stop worrying about your looks.'

'It's okay for you. You don't have any obvious defects.'

At that, she fell silent for a moment. He had a point. And she liked what his observation implied. He couldn't think of anything he didn't like about her appearance. That surely led to the conclusion he found her attractive? Wrinkling her nose, she moved forward again, giggling at his suspicious look. It was so much fun putting him on edge. He needed to be distracted from all that was worrying him.

This time he didn't step away, but his expression was wary. 'You're right, Bonnie. God doesn't make mistakes. He has allowed me to look this way, but it's all a result of sin messing up the world. We live in a fallen world.'

'Oh, Blaze.' Bonnie laughed as she bent to pick up the pile of horse manure she had carefully stepped over earlier, 'I happen to live in a different world from you and mine's perfect. But I know how to deal with your pimples. In fact, I think we can make them totally disappear.'

Blaze quirked an eyebrow at her, backing away until she had him in a corner. Her arm came up, but with speed and strength that amazed her, he grabbed her wrist and spun her around, forcing her arm behind her back. He growled in her ear and she could hear the smile in his voice.

'Drop it!'

'Not until you concede defeat.'

He sputtered out a laugh. 'What?'

'You heard me.'

He spun her back around to see her face, then unclenched her fingers one by until she dropped the manure. The remains were still on her hand and she eyed it for a moment before looking back at him, her intentions clear.

'Don't you dare, Miss Perfect.' Blaze chuckled. 'Come near me with that and you'll end up with it all over your perfect little face. And maybe even some in your mouth just to teach you not to mess with me.'

Bonnie never could resist a challenge. She lunged forward but had no hope. He was laughing as he held her off. She finally relaxed, seeing that the worried crease had gone from his brow. It had been worth it just to see him smile again. She smiled back into his eyes until he let her hands go. He seemed breathless despite the effortlessness of holding her off. She didn't move away, but just stood grinning at him. She saw the way red crept up his neck and into his cheeks. He stepped back quickly and avoided her eyes. There it was again; his obvious discomfort at her touch. His smile had disappeared and the frown of concern had returned.

'Bonnie, I long for you to believe, but I just don't know what it will take. What will make you see your need?'

She shrugged, sincerely doubting she had a need. Perhaps if she had a need she would believe in God. But for now, she was content – content with everything except the way her unbelief caused Blaze such pain. She reached out her dirty hand toward him. 'Come on, I'll walk you back to the fence line.'

'Okay, but I'm not stupid enough to hold your hand.'

She grinned and let it fall back to her side. He was smiling again. That was an achievement. It amused her to see the way he shoved his hands in his pockets.

'I don't know much about the Bible yet.' He glanced at her as they walked. 'But when I know more, I want to share it with you. And something I do know is that God only lets bad things happen if He can work good out of them. Everything happens for a reason, even in a fallen world.'

Bonnie's look was sceptical. 'You reckon?'

'I'm sure. It says in the Bible that He works everything together for our good if we believe in Him.'

She chuckled. 'I guess we need to have reasons for our beliefs. If you feel more comfortable with the world believing that the bad is really good, that's fine by me.'

Blaze shook his dark head in frustration. 'What if I'm wrong? What if we just live for the now and after we die, that's it. What have I lost?'

'Nothing.' Bonnie didn't like where this was headed.

'But what have *you* lost if I'm right?'

He was right. She would lose everything, including life. But she simply didn't believe like he did. That's all there was to it.

'Bonnie, I can't bear the thought of you going to hell.' He had stopped and reached for her shoulders. She could hear the pain in his voice. 'And I hate that you don't know God like I do and I hate that you live without purpose.'

She knew this was no time to play with him. 'I wish I could say I believe,' she admitted softly, 'but I don't. I know you believe with all your heart, but Blaze, I don't.'

He nodded. 'I don't want you to say you believe when you don't. I just wish I knew what else I can do.'

Chapter Ten

Bonnie decided the Clements family needed a distraction. She had always longed to ride the magnificent Victorian Dream and there she stood, totally saddled in the yard and all alone. The surprised horse stood perfectly still as Bonnie climbed the fence beside her, stood on the top rail and then scrambled awkwardly into the saddle from the fence. Her respect for Misty was renewed as she recalled the nimble circus girl leaping directly onto the horse from the ground. How she managed to do it, Bonnie had no idea.

Sitting atop the large creature gave Bonnie an incredible feeling of power. She longed to race the wind, feeling the strength of the horse's muscles moving beneath her. Excitement raced through her veins as she leaned forward in the saddle and spoke into Victorian Dream's ear.

'Want to run?'

The horse whinnied in response.

'Hey!' a voice called in surprise from the paddock nearby. 'Bonnie?'

'Quick, Victorian.' Bonnie nudged the horse with the toe of her shoe. 'We have to move now or we won't get our run.' With that, she moved the horse into a canter, then a gallop. With so little experience, it was very hard to keep her balance on the large creature, but somehow she managed. She gave a shout and relaxed as she felt the wind surging through her hair. This was the exhilarating feeling she had longed for!

Out of the corner of her eye Bonnie saw Storm running toward Blaze's caravan. 'Blaze, that idiot friend of yours has taken off on VD!'

Bonnie chuckled, wondering why Storm insisted on calling the horse by the name that infuriated Misty. Misty didn't want her horse to sound more like some form of disease than the majestic creature she was.

Bonnie looked back and saw Blaze fling down the book he was holding and run toward her. She didn't know what they were all so worried about. She had meant to distract them, not upset them. Maybe it was best to turn back.

Worried looks from the family met Bonnie as she brought Victorian Dream into the yard and circled her.

'She's pretty good for a beginner,' Misty commented and Bonnie could hear the admiration in her voice.

'She's wild!' Storm contradicted, followed by a string of swear words. Yet he couldn't keep the admiration from his eyes, either. Bonnie knew courage always impressed him, whether or not it was responsible.

Blaze was not so calm as he rushed toward her, his voice loud and angry. 'Bonnie, what do you think you're doing?'

She merely grinned as she lowered herself from the huge horse.

'Aren't you afraid of anything?' He led her away from the stunned family who were checking Victorian Dream over; apart from Starre, who was staring after them, mouth open. Bonnie enjoyed the attention and chuckled.

'No. You've asked me that before.' She nudged his riding

boot with her shoe. 'Stop stressing. I had everything under perfect control.'

'Maybe. But what if she got a fright? Controlling an animal like that takes experience and what if you'd fallen or been thrown? What if …'

Bonnie silenced him by reaching a hand to his cheek. 'Are you saying you were frightened for me, Blaze?'

He threw her hand from his cheek. 'What do you think?' He turned his back.

Not fooled by his tone, Bonnie waited for him to look at her again. When he turned back the anger had gone and all she could see was the concern that shone in his eyes. She knew in that moment that he cared for her. Deeply. He was incredible, the way he cared for his family; the way he stood by his convictions and lived with compassion. Bonnie recognised then, that what she felt for him had grown much deeper than friendship.

'Blaze,' she said, almost breathlessly. 'I love you!'

He could not have looked more surprised. She loved the way he stared at her, confusion washing over his face for a moment. Then he shook his head in angry frustration. 'Don't tease.'

She knew the moment he realised she was serious. His eyes deepened and he swallowed hard. He opened his mouth as though about to say something, then closed it again. She had a strong urge to kiss that mouth. She longed to hold him and have him melt at her touch. What was happening to her? She reached a hand and rested it on his pimple covered cheek.

'I know we believe different things but that doesn't matter to me anymore.'

Blaze shook his head, eyes filled with regret. Gently this time, he removed her hand from his cheek.

'It matters to me, Bonnie. Living for God is my life and purpose. I can't share my life with someone who's going in the opposite direction. It wouldn't work.'

'But Blaze, I know you could love me. It would be crazy to let religion come between us.'

Blaze shook his head again, his eyes shadowed. 'No, Bonnie,' was all he would say. 'I've got to go.'

'Wait! Blaze.' She was pleading with him now.

He turned back. 'Bonnie, you have to understand it just wouldn't work. I'm flattered that you have feelings for me. I've never had popular, attractive girls flirt with me.' He blushed even as he said the words. 'Or even want to be friends with me. But unless you believe … well, even though I've prayed for it day and night I just can't see that happening? Can you?'

Slowly, she shook her head and he shrugged. 'Sometimes we have to let go of dreams and live in reality … no matter what it costs us.' He headed back to the caravans and Bonnie followed a few steps behind. Her heart confused, she considered turning around and heading straight back home. Or maybe she needed to run after Blaze – make him change his mind. She took a step in his direction when Starre appeared from nowhere.

'Bonnie, I've got to talk to you.'

Her tone was urgent and Bonnie knew she would have to put aside her own hurt for a moment. Blaze had entered his caravan without so much as a glance back and Starre needed her full attention.

'Marcos returned Steadfast Ever.' Starre pulled at her shirt sleeves, stretching them in her agitation. 'He just turned up with Steadfast in a horse float and pretended he was concerned I would be missing him. But as soon as Johnny wasn't listening he told me he will make sure Blaze gets hurt if I don't hurry up and get the signatures on the contract. I couldn't stand it if anything happened to Blaze and Marcos knows it!

Bonnie's eyes widened in dismay. 'Oh, Starre, I'm sorry. We've got to put an end to this. You really have to go to the police.'

Starre took in a quivering breath. 'Can you come with me?'

Bonnie recognised fear and nodded. Anything to put an end to this awful drama. So, on the back of Steadfast Ever, they rode to the police station. A different man stood at the front desk and he seemed more professional than the last. He took down Starre's story, asking questions and comforting the girl as much as possible.

'Make sure you always have someone with you wherever you go,' he told Starre as they prepared to leave. 'It's not that I believe this man will put you in any real danger, but it's a sensible precaution to take. And if anything happens, the more witnesses the better.'

'And you'll look into this?' Bonnie checked.

He nodded. 'Yes. No threat of kidnapping should be taken lightly. Don't you worry, we'll sort this out.'

Bonnie breathed a sigh of relief. Being friends with the Clements family was giving her an anxiety she had never known before. Yet she wouldn't miss their friendship for anything. It was all worth it just to know them and be a part of their extraordinary world. And she wasn't worried about Blaze. She would win him over eventually.

Chapter Eleven

Bonnie glanced around the school yard. Blaze normally waited for her, but today he was nowhere to be seen. There was a group of students hanging around the gate. She approached, watching as one slipped something into his pocket. The pocket now bulged suspiciously in the shape of a cigarette packet.

'Have you seen Blaze?'

The one with the box in his pocket shook his head.

'No, but there's a guy looking for you.'

'A guy? What guy?'

'Some bald bloke. I saw him talking to Starre Clements, but she ran off. Then the guy asked us if we had seen you.' He grinned. 'Gave us – well, something – for saying you were on your way home.'

Bonnie frowned. 'But I'm not.'

'So? He wasn't to know that, was he?'

Bonnie was disgusted at the student who had obviously gained a packet of cigarettes for his lie. Distracted, she glanced around. Who would be looking for her? She turned back to face the student who was still looking pleased with himself.

'Did you tell the guy where I live?'

'No, but Brad told him what way you normally go.'

Trust Brad. Bonnie decided to take a different way home. She jogged out the gate, missing Blaze's presence beside her, but aware that his company had prevented her from training for athletics each day on the way home. As she passed the showground, she stared in surprise at the row of trucks parked on the grounds. She glanced around and then noticed one of the trucks was pulling out onto the road behind her. It began moving slowly and in a moment of unease she realised it was following her! The knowledge gave her an eerie feeling and she recognised then, for the first time in her life, she was afraid. There was a bold sign painted on the side of the truck. It read, 'Marcos' Circus'.

Bonnie knew then that she was in trouble. She began to run faster, looking for an escape. The truck came up beside her. The only escape would be to run across the show ground right into the circus camp. Surely there were enough trucks there for her to hide behind? She glanced back. The truck on the road had stopped. Two men jumped out and began to run in her direction. If she could just reach that line of trucks—

Thump! Bonnie's breath left her. She'd run straight into a large, fierce looking man who came out from behind one of the trucks. Instinctively she knew this man was Marcos. From now her every word and move would count.

Despite her fear, Bonnie forced herself to think rationally. She needed to distract them, convince them they had found the wrong person. Then she had to make a dash for it. She stood taller, glared at the man who blocked her way.

'What's going on?'

The man didn't appear the least bit intimidated. He grabbed her arm in a grip that hurt. 'Are you Bonnie, Blaze's friend?'

'Blaze? Who's Blaze?' She thought she acted very well, but clearly they weren't convinced.

'Starre tells me you helped them write statements against us.' The man's eyebrows closed together in a threatening way.

'Statements?' Bonnie fought a wave of panic. Starre? Had she confessed everything to these men?

One of the men stepped closer. She felt trapped, tried to keep calm.

'Don't bother trying to mess with us.' He grabbed her other arm. 'They've cheated us and nobody gets away with that. We want our horses back.'

'I don't know what you're talking about!' Bonnie was annoyed by the tremor she could hear in her voice. She'd just broken one of the Ten Commandments by lying. What a bizarre thought to come at a time like this. Blaze and his beliefs were clearly getting to her.

'No?' The man raised his eyebrow. 'We'll see about that.' He dragged her to a solidly built truck and shoved her forward as he opened the back. Bonnie gasped when she looked in. There inside was Blaze, his hands tied. He looked shocked to see her.

'Bonnie! What happened?'

Marcos laughed. 'Blaze?' he mocked. ' Who's Blaze?' He shoved her into the truck while she struggled. She managed to give one of them a good bite on the arm, but to no avail.

'Now, you two can just cuddle up in here for a while and we'll get on with our business.' Marcos turned away, then turned back to say, 'Oh, Bonnie, while you're in there, you might want to think about asking Starre Clements to retract her statement against us. We don't want any police involved. Maybe you could even convince Blaze his God isn't helping him anymore.' He laughed again. 'Then you can convince your friends they better give us the horses, with signed legal documents saying they are ours.'

She glanced at Blaze. He seemed extremely relaxed

considering he was tied up inside a circus truck. The door slammed closed, leaving them in total, smothering blackness. Bonnie was glad for Blaze's presence, but wished she could see him.

'Can you untie me?' His calm voice seemed loud in the darkness. Bonnie wondered if she could control her shaking hands enough to have a go, but knew she had to try. She came toward where she remembered he had been sitting, and heard his breathing. It was steady, nothing like her own fast, shallow breaths.

'Are you okay?' His voice was closer than she expected.

'Yeah, just a bit shaken.'

She began to work at the rope, wondering if Blaze had any idea what being so close to him did to her already racing pulse. If he could feel the way she shook, he didn't comment. She wished he would speak again; tell her what he was thinking. If he wouldn't end this awful, black silence she would have to think of something to say.

'It's fairly tight,' was all she could come up with.

'I know. Circus people are brilliant with knots.'

Finally, she gave up. Her hands were red and sore where rope burns had formed. The cold of the truck was beginning to creep into her skin and she shook harder.

'Lean close. It will keep us both warm,' Blaze instructed gently. Cautiously, she did, careful not to lean as close as she wanted to. The closer she was, the more he would be aware of her fear and it shamed her. She was not one to be afraid. She prided herself on her courage and determination.

'You'll have to come closer than that.' Blaze laughed, but it sounded a little forced. 'Don't worry, I have clean clothes on.'

She chuckled with him. It sounded hollow even to her own ears. She allowed herself to snuggle into him and drew in the warmth of his body. Finally her shivering lessened.

'They can't keep us here without the police finding out, can they?'

She felt Blaze shake his head. 'I don't think so, but it could take a while for the police to find us.'

Her concern grew as she felt the coldness more deeply. 'Can't you pray that we'll get out of here?'

'Don't worry, I have been.'

'Will you pray so I can hear?' She needed the comfort of hearing him talk to his God. Even if he was surprised by her request, Blaze obliged. His voice trembled slightly but began to calm as he prayed. The sound of his steady voice as he spoke to God with familiarity helped to take away some of the blackness there in the truck. Blaze asked his God for peace as well as some way of escape out of the whole mess.

As Bonnie leaned against his chest, she could hear his deep voice rumbling in her ear. She could also feel the comforting, steady beat of his heart. At that moment she didn't mind if she didn't ever get out of there – so long as Blaze was with her. Shocked by her own irrational thoughts in the midst of being kidnapped, she sat up.

'Bonnie?' Blaze sounded concerned.

Her movements were fast as she began working again on the ropes that bound him. 'I'm okay.' She was determined to fight her fear; fight these circus people who dared do this to Blaze and his family.

'They're starting to feel loose,' Blaze encouraged. 'You're doing a good job.'

Bonnie smiled at his encouragement. Finally, a knot came loose. Then another and another until Bonnie stood with a shout of victory. He was free! Blaze jumped to his feet and gave her a fierce hug as he laughed low in his chest.

'You might want to keep your voice down.'

Bonnie covered her mouth with her hand, triumph draining from her. 'Oops.' It was true. They weren't truly free. Not yet. There was no way to get out of that truck. They sat back down, drawing from one another's warmth. It was nice to have him reach his arms around her now he was untied. There was no hesitation in his touch and Bonnie wondered if it was the darkness that hid his usual awkwardness, or if something had changed. Was God giving him extra confidence and strength the way he had prayed a few minutes ago?

'Blaze?'

'Yeah?'

'Why are those circus guys so angry that you believe in God?'

He sighed, smoothed back her hair before resting his chin on her head. It felt protective and big brotherly. She wondered if he even realised what he was doing.

'When I became a Christian, it stirred up a hornet's' nest right through the circus. And when I lost interest in circus riding, Johnny began to think maybe we all needed an education. Apparently our mother never wanted any of us to grow up in the circus. She died having the twins, so she didn't have much say in it. Johnny started to remember what Mum wanted for us and wanted to honour her wishes. So, we left and Marcos blamed me. He says there's no place for God in his circus – and he's right.'

'So how did you become a Christian, then?'

'One night after a show a girl was hanging around our horses, Storm went off at her but she was just interested in the horses because her dad breeds thoroughbreds. Anyway, I got talking with her and she told me all about God and her beliefs. I wanted to know more so I started going to churches in whatever town we were in, bought a whole lot of books about God and started reading. Shelley had given me her father's business card in case we were interested in getting more horses, so I used the contact details to keep in touch with her. Since then we've kept in contact and she encourages me in my walk with God. I've learned so much from her!'

Bonnie noticed the tone in his voice as he spoke of Shelley and felt a twinge of jealousy. Shelley believed as Blaze did. What was to stop them taking their relationship further? Was there already something going on between them?

'I've told Shelley about you and she prays for you, too.'

Bonnie was glad he couldn't see her expression. The last thing she wanted was a girlfriend of Blaze's praying for her. She considered telling him, but stopped as noises came from outside. The door opened and light flooded in. Blaze and Bonnie shielded their eyes to see the man standing there.

Blaze recognised him. 'Marcos, there's no reason for you to hold Bonnie here. Can't you let her go?'

Marcos nodded. 'Exactly my intentions, boy. I just wanted her to know how serious we are. You can go now, both of you.'

Her arm brushed against Blaze's as they edged out of the truck. He felt cold to the touch. What could they do? These men had no qualms about carrying out their threats. There was no way the Clements family would give up their horses or return to the circus when Marcos had treated them this way. Surely he knew his plan wouldn't work? If only the police could stop all this.

'Let's get home as quickly as possible!' Blaze whispered urgently. 'Marcos is up to something.' They rushed out into the dusk and a few moments later Blaze hailed a passing driver who stopped to pick them up.

As they rounded the bend and the Clements' caravans came into view, a strange glow shone from over the hill where Bonnie knew the stables to be. Then she saw people surrounding the gateway where a man was loading Starre's horse into a float.

Lined up behind were Victorian Dream and Montford Express.

Blaze's body became like a coiled spring ready for action. He jumped out of the vehicle the moment it stopped.

'No, don't! Leave them!' he yelled while Bonnie hurriedly thanked the puzzled driver and explained what was happening at the same time.

'Keep back!' the large man beside the horse float told Blaze in a threatening tone.

'Everything's under way now. You are going to tell the police that your precious horses died right there in that stable. Got it?'

As Blaze ran to the horse float, Bonnie struggled to understand the man's words. She ran to the top of the rise to where the strange orange glow was growing brighter by the second. What she saw made her gasp and stop short. The stables were on fire! Beauty was also on the rise, motionless, just staring. Bonnie rushed to her. She looked totally dazed and lost. Bonnie grabbed the girl's arms and spun her around.

'Beauty, what's happening?' Bonnie had never seen such fear or pain in anybody's expression before in her life.

Chapter Twelve

'Regal Zion is in there!' Beauty screamed, started running around in circles.

'Prince's horse?' Bonnie felt her heart beat faster and her body tense for action as Beauty gave the answer.

'Yes! He's going to be burned alive!'

Beauty was hysterical. Through Bonnie's mind flashed the reaction on Prince's face when he learned his beloved Regal Zion had been burned. She couldn't let it happen. These creatures were family to these people. Hearing Regal Zion's terrified whinny, she simply couldn't bear to let him burn, either. Without further thought for her own safety, she forced the screaming Beauty to sit down and ran toward the stable.

The heat was incredible. She had never been so close to such a fire before. Ignoring the hissing and roaring of the flames she raced into the building. There, through the haze of smoke, Regal Zion jumped up and down, his eyes wild with fright.

'It's okay, I'm coming to get you out,' Bonnie promised the desperate horse, wondering even as she spoke the words if it were possible.

She struggled to see. Her eyes already streamed with tears from the smoke. With urgent moves she tugged at the rope holding the horse fast. The more she tried to hurry, the more she fumbled and felt she was getting nowhere.

'Relax, Bonnie. Focus. Think.'

Finally the frantic horse was free. He rushed past, kicking Bonnie in the shin and knocked her down. Pain shot through her leg but she refused to look at the damage.

'I have to get out of here!' She spoke through gritted teeth, trying to ignore the pain, the awful, smothering smoke and the fire eating up the wooden building before her very eyes. She struggled to move. Why couldn't she lift that leg? Her hand reached down. Something warm and sticky trickled through her fingers. Blood? No time to look now. She had to force herself to keep going.

The intense heat seemed to burn holes through her skin. Every nerve tingled with the awful sensation. How long did it take for people to be burned to death? She had no idea it would be such agony. Struggling through the flashes of light and choking heat, she gasped in pain as a flame lapped against her leg. She was alight! This awful fire was feeding on her skin! Would it be easier to keep struggling, or just let herself go peacefully? Too tired to struggle ... anymore ...?

The crackling of the flames and the falling timber was so loud, the flames so bright she could neither hear nor see. In that moment she knew she did not want to die alone. She couldn't bear to think of her mother and father hearing she'd been burnt to death. And she didn't want Blaze to grieve because he had not convinced her of the truth as he saw it. Blaze would believe she had gone to hell ... couldn't bear to put him through that agony. She must fight. If ... any chance ... must fight.

Exhaustion almost overcame her. She fought it off, dragged herself through the flames. At last, fresh air against her skin. On grass at last. Helpless and horrified at what she had just come through.

Crawling as close to the ground as possible had saved her life. The choking sensation of smoke threatened to suffocate her. The smell of burning was dreadful. Yet she couldn't move.

Faintly, somewhere in the haze of her mind, she could hear voices. She recognised Blaze's voice. It was horrified and demanding all at once.

'You let Bonnie go in there?'

'Regal Zion was in there,' Beauty was reasoning through pathetic sobs.

'I can't believe you could be so stupid!' Blaze's voice was hoarse from the smoke and fear combined. 'She's human, Beauty. Regal Zion is just a horse.'

Bonnie tried to call out. All her dry throat could provide was a horrible, painful croak. She began to swirl into blackness.

'Bonnie? Bonnie? … Oh no, Johnny, quick, over here!'

She felt Blaze's hands as he grasped her arms and gasped at the sight of her. She was too tired to respond. Every ounce of strength was needed just to take her next breath.

'Bonnie, if you're with us, can you squeeze my hand?' She didn't recognise that voice, but squeezed, then fell into blackness once more.

* * *

Burned and dazed, Bonnie woke in hospital a week later to find her mother by the bedside. The hand that reached to brush hair back from her forehead was tentative, almost as though not daring to hope.

'Bonnie, are you awake?'

She managed a nod. That pain seared through her again. Bonnie allowed her eyes to close for a moment before fighting to open them. Her throat and chest hurt terribly, an even greater pain clutched her arms and legs. She could hardly bear it and wished she could return to the nothingness.

'We knew you'd make it.' Mrs Blake's voice was tight with emotion as she continued to stroke her daughter's forehead as if afraid she might break.

Bonnie listened to her mother's voice. Heard how she'd been taken by helicopter from one hospital to another. Now, finally it seemed she would make it. After skin grafts, intensive care and much prayer from Blaze, his friend Shelley and the people of Blaze's church, they all believed she would survive.

It was then it all came back to Bonnie. The fire. The pain and desperation. Blaze thinking she'd died. How could Blaze even imagine hell was one continual fire?

'Mr Seton has been a wonderful support.'

Mr Seton? Bonnie searched her hazy mind. He was Rachel Seton's father, wasn't he? Yes, the minister of the church Blaze attended.

'He's come in every day and …' Mrs Blake's voice faded out as Bonnie's tired eyes closed once more and blackness came over her in a wave.

***

'Bonnie, Bonnie it's me.'

At the sound of her father's voice, Bonnie forced herself to make a way through the blackness and into consciousness. She opened heavy-lidded eyes to witness her father cry for the first time in her life. Gently he took her bandaged hand.

His voice was husky. 'Thank you for fighting!' He swallowed hard, his eyes wet. 'I knew if anyone could survive this, you could!'

Bonnie felt nothing except the pain consuming her body. Her heart blank, she listened, realising she was different. Never before had there been such emptiness and lack of emotion in her. There was a nothingness somewhere deep inside. Her father seemed to sense the change and grasped her hand.

'I love you, Bonnie!'

She managed a nod. She knew. But this pain was worse than anything she'd ever experienced and she wished she could die. No, not die. She was too afraid to die. She wished she had never been born, had never existed. Anything to escape this unrelenting torment.

The agony overwhelmed her. She tossed and turned in an attempt to find some relief. She vaguely heard her parents begging the nurses to do something. But nothing more could be done and she just had to bear it. If only she had discovered the truth about God, then she could have stopped fighting. She could have confidently submitted to the darkness that wanted to claim her and die in peace.

'Hang in there, Bonnie.' Her father was now pleading. 'Don't give in.'

Bonnie gritted her teeth. She had no choice.

Gradually she learned to bear the pain. And slowly – terribly slowly, it lessened.

* * *

Bonnie had no idea how many days or weeks had passed. At times she would listen to the clock ticking, willing it forward to a time when all this would be just a bad memory. At other times she wanted to yank it from the wall and smash it on the ground. Yet she didn't have the strength.

A nurse stepped into the room. 'The Clements family to see you, Bonnie.'

Bonnie simply nodded, still feeling nothing. The family filed in and she carefully hid her hands and arms beneath the sheets. They didn't need to see the bandages or the skin peeling off her.

It was repulsive. If it made her want to be sick, what would it do to them? She didn't have the energy to lift her head from the pillow, couldn't bring herself to smile. She hated the sorrow and pity on the faces of her visitors hesitating as they saw her.

There was an awkward silence. Then to Bonnie's surprise, Misty took the lead. She came to the bedside, rested a hand on the bed and looked directly into Bonnie's eyes.

'It's so good to see you. We were so worried about you. How are you going?'

Bonnie shrugged. 'I'm alive.'

Her voice was still hoarse from smoke inhalation and her tone blunt and humourless. She might have said more, but at that moment she glanced behind Misty and saw Beauty. The look on the girl's face stopped her. Beauty's whole expression was filled with horror and guilt. The shame written on her face shadowed her whole appearance. Had the family blamed Beauty for the accident or was she torturing herself with the blame? She needed to reassure the poor girl.

'It's okay, Beauty.' She tried to sit up but failed. 'It was my choice to go in. Even if you hadn't told me to, I couldn't have let Regal Zion die.'

Beauty nodded slightly, her expression unchanged but a small light came into her eyes. Feeling overwhelmed with tiredness, Bonnie felt her eyes slide shut before she even looked around at the rest of the family.

Chapter Thirteen

The rehabilitation was hard work. Pain was so constant and tiring. The nurses were very understanding and helpful, but it was really Bonnie's parents who brought her through the worst of it. Their encouragement was endless, their joy at her achievements motivating. Finally, after months of work and further surgery, she was ready to go home.

'We'll miss you, Bonnie.' The nurse hovering around Bonnie had a genuine look of regret. Then she shrugged and smiled. 'No one has ever been sorry to leave this place, though. Finally you are free to live your own life again and maybe even sleep in! I won't be waking you up at six every morning to take your blood pressure.'

Bonnie liked the friendly young nurse and settled back into the bed to enjoy her chatter.

'Bonnie, are you respectable?' one of the wardsmen interrupted from the door.

'Yes! I'm always respectable.' She gave him a cheeky grin. 'In fact, I would say I am so respected by most people that I am admired.'

She stopped short. Blaze Clements was standing behind the wardsman. She hadn't seen him since the day his family had taken that long trip to visit her in the city hospital soon after she had come out of her coma.

The wardsman stepped aside and motioned to Blaze. 'You're right to go in, mate.'

Bonnie took in a deep breath while the nurse stepped discreetly closer. 'Wow, why don't I get visitors who look like that? Oh, that's right. I'm not a patient, so I don't get to soak up the sympathy of good looking young men.'

Despite the heaviness in her heart, Bonnie grinned. The nurse left, and Bonnie found herself uncomfortably alone with Blaze. His look was too penetrating and she wished he would relax and be light-hearted. She didn't think she could handle his preaching right now. But then, she thought, maybe she needed it. Maybe Blaze had some answers. Suddenly she desperately needed answers and she knew she couldn't let Blaze go until she had them. She met his eyes unflinchingly, hiding her burned hands under the sheet.

'Do you still believe in your God, Blaze?' She hadn't meant it to come out quite so challenging and wished she had at least said hello first. But she couldn't take it back now and she really did need answers. She watched the way he swallowed hard. He opened his mouth as though about to say something, then turned his face away without answering. Frustration rose up in Bonnie.

'Well? Do you?' Anger she didn't even know existed was springing from somewhere deep inside. 'Do you believe a God of love could let this happen? Do you still believe everything you kept preaching at me? You're deluded if you think a God of love could send anybody through a fire on earth, let alone an eternal one!'

He turned back and Bonnie stifled a gasp at the pain in his eyes. 'I'm struggling.' His confession was so quiet she barely heard him.

Bonnie stared at him in shock, sorry for her anger. He didn't deserve it. It all made sense now; his desperation for her to believe; his insistence on talking about his faith. She wouldn't want her worst enemy to go through what she had, let alone a friend. And if Blaze didn't believe, who would? She needed someone to explain this to her; to give her a reason for what happened! How she needed someone who believed in God!

The sadness in Blaze's eyes broke her heart as he turned and walked from the room without another word. The regret Bonnie felt was almost too much to bear. Why had she challenged his faith so harshly? He had made the effort to come and see her and her insensitivity had sent him away. Lying back against the pillows in defeat, Bonnie wondered what she could have been thinking. Where was Blaze? He was probably already on his way back to Everdeen.

The morning seemed to last forever as Bonnie waited for the final paperwork that would allow her to go home. She had been waiting for this day for so long and now suddenly she didn't feel prepared. Everything was so complicated. She gazed in the mirror the nurses had provided and tried to brush the tangles from her hair. The hospital bed had a way of creating more knots than running in the wind had ever managed. As she gazed at her reflection, she began to appreciate what Blaze might have thought, looking at her. She was not physically attractive anymore.

'I'm really ugly,' she acknowledged sadly as she stared at that dreadful image. 'I can't stand how I look. Nobody should have to look at something so … so awful.'

She studied the withered skin on her hands then started as she heard Blaze's deep voice come softly from behind. 'Want some help?'

He had returned! Unable to respond, except to flame with shame that he had seen the scars on her hands, Bonnie watched him approach in the mirror. Gently he took the brush from her burned hand and began to work through the tangles in her hair. He worked in silence for quite a while, as Bonnie tried to think of an apology. He broke the silence before she had perfected her speech.

'I'm glad the fire didn't get your face.' His voice was gruff, but his expression was almost tender. 'You still look like the old you.'

'My face does,' she acknowledged, 'but the rest of me …' She shrugged, but it was not the familiar, carefree shrug of the old Bonnie. 'Well, now I know my need like you and your friend Shelley prayed I would.' She gave a dry smile. 'Life isn't perfect anymore and I know I have needs.'

Blaze put down the brush and stepped out of view in the mirror. Bonnie turned to look at him directly and saw his eyes were burning with emotion.

'If I'd known this is how God would do it, I would never have prayed such a prayer!' He seemed to be accusing God as he looked upward. Immediately Bonnie's regret deepened.

'Don't let this take your faith.' Her voice came out in an urgent whisper. 'Please, Blaze. Don't let what happened to me change you, too. Enough damage has already been done.'

When Blaze looked back to her, she caught the glisten of tears in his eyes. He reached out and took her scarred hand and studied it, gently touching the wrinkled skin.

'I'm finding this all so hard, Bonnie. Seeing you lying there and thinking God let you die without believing. And even when I realised you were alive, I just felt so angry with God. I can't believe he let this happen to you! How *could* He?'

Bonnie gave a rueful smile. 'I guess it's like you said. God gives us a choice. He never forces us to do anything. I chose to go into that fire. And I chose not to believe.'

Blaze shook his head. 'But did you really choose not to believe? You told me yourself you would believe if you could! Why didn't God prove Himself to you? I know He can! He did to me! Why did He not choose to show you, Bonnie? That's what gets me. If He really loved you as much as ... if He really loved you He would show you.'

Bonnie felt she understood, but could find no words to respond. She looked down at his unblemished hand holding hers. Blaze had nice hands. They were strong, manly hands. Why had she never noticed before? Was it because she was so horribly aware her own hands were no longer nice? That they made her feel sick to the stomach? Blaze let go of her hand to push a strand of hair from her face. His eyes reflected the pain he felt.

His voice was hoarse. 'It was all so quick, Bonnie. I was too busy worrying about saving those wretched horses to think about where you were. That horse-focused life was the life I left when I became a Christian but it came back so quickly. And Beauty ... well, I have to keep forgiving her over and over. She could have stopped you, too.'

Bonnie unthinkingly took his other hand into hers, scars forgotten for a moment, 'Didn't you once tell me God forgives if you ask him to? And you said that not accepting his forgiveness is throwing it back in his face. Is that what you're doing?'

He fell silent as he took in her question and then slowly he began to smile. A beautiful, complete smile.

'I guess I have been,' he admitted, 'but I'm the preacher, Bonnie, not you!'

Bonnie smiled, too, and found it made her pale cheeks ache. Perhaps, she hoped, perhaps one day, things would go back to how they were before the fire.

Chapter Fourteen

Bonnie had only been home a few days when Misty came to visit. Hearing her familiar voice speaking with her mother at the door, Bonnie listened for Blaze. To her disappointment, Misty walked in alone. It might seem rude to ask after Blaze straight away, but Bonnie couldn't help herself. She had to know. Pushing herself up on her elbows she gave Misty a half-hearted smile.

'Blaze didn't come?'

Misty cleared her throat and looked uncomfortable as the smile faded from her dimpled face.

'Nah … um, had homework to do.'

Homework? It was clearly an excuse and Bonnie felt her heart sink. Was it her burns? Her appearance? Memories? Something she had said when he came to the hospital? Misty sat in a chair beside her and Bonnie attempted to put thoughts of Blaze aside. Misty had come to visit and she should be grateful for that. 'So what's been happening?'

Misty brightened and her dimpled smile returned. 'They caught Marcos and returned the horses.'

'So it's all over?'

'Yep. The policeman said they're not likely to bully us again.' Misty chattered on and Bonnie listened silently to the details of the months she had missed. She lay on the lounge trying to be interested and light-hearted but failing miserably. Misty's cheerful chatter simply reminded her of all she had missed and that life would never be the same again.

'You'll never guess – we're moving into a house!' Misty didn't seem to notice Bonnie's deepening despondency. 'The fire burned a couple of the caravans so Johnny decided it's time we live like a normal family. The house is huge! It has four bedrooms. I'm going to share with Starre, and Beauty can have a room to herself. She's impossible to live with so she'll have to put up with being alone.'

Thinking of Misty's rough, reckless ways, Bonnie's mouth turned up slightly. Beauty had done herself a favour by being 'impossible'. It wouldn't be much fun sharing a room where no one could move without tripping over clothes and riding gear strewn across the floor.

'Blaze is keeping his caravan, and Storm and Prince are sharing a room.' Misty bubbled with excitement. 'Johnny has made up a cleaning roster because there's rules about renting or something.'

'Yeah, there are.' Bonnie agreed dryly. For the first time she didn't find Misty's ignorance about everyday life and hygiene amusing. In fact, she was feeling so tense she just wished Misty would leave. However, Misty had stopped and seemed to be waiting for Bonnie to say something. Straining her mind, she finally came up with a question.

'So where are you keeping the horses now?'

'Still at Collagg's Waterfall for now. When the property sale goes through, we'll lease the paddock behind the house for them. We are going to build new stables – even bigger ones – so we can fit Blaze's horse in.'

'Blaze's horse?' Bonnie frowned in confusion. 'Blaze doesn't have a horse.'

Misty looked awkward for a moment. 'Oh yeah, I forgot. That happened while you were in hospital. Shelley gave Blaze a horse.'

'Shelley?'

'Yeah, a friend he met after a circus performance one night. Her family breed horses and she knows more about them than anyone I know … except us, of course.'

Bonnie knew very well who Shelley was. It was the fact that she had given Blaze such a gift that bothered her. A horse was not something you would give to anyone unless they meant a lot to you. An awful lot. She'd tried to convince Blaze to get a horse and failed. Why had Shelley succeeded?

'Guess what he named it?'

'Hallelujah? Divine Providence?'

Misty grinned and Bonnie knew she had totally missed the sarcasm in her answer. 'No, Peter Pan. It really suits him. He's an amazing horse, huge and fast. Even more valuable than Victorian Dream.'

Peter Pan? Blaze had used the name she had recommended? Somehow the knowledge that Blaze had remembered her when naming the horse, brought relief.

* * *

The days dragged by, and Bonnie found she was able to walk short distances around the house without feeling dizzy and weak. Mostly she lay across the lounge in front of the television. She had seen every television commercial numerous times now and they were irritating her. Even the television shows weren't interesting anymore. She felt ready to socialise.

'Mum, do you know why Belinda hasn't come to see me yet?'

Mrs Blake looked up from the dress she was ironing then

set the iron down. She waited until Bonnie turned from the television to actually look at her. 'There could be any number of reasons ...'

Bonnie chuckled but it was a hollow sound. 'She's probably too busy having to organise two speeches for every debate.'

'Or she's scared. Facing the unknown frightens some people.'

Bonnie's eyes clouded at her mother's quiet comment. 'What do you mean?'

'She knows you're different, Bonnie. There was a picture in the paper and the whole story was on the news.'

'A picture?' Bonnie jumped up, her heart racing. 'You don't mean the cameras got to the scene of the fire?'

'No, but they got to the hospital.'

'And you let them in?' Bonnie's voice had become high pitched in her panic. Her mother's calm nature made her feel worse.

'No, I didn't let them in. It's very hard to stop some reporters.'

Bonnie lowered herself back into the lounge chair. Dizziness washed over her. She forced her shaking hands to her side. 'What did the picture show?'

The commercials were over, the movie was back on, but no one was taking any notice. Bonnie waited, her mother's hesitation telling her the truth she dreaded knowing. Eyes closed, she listened to her mother's slow steps into the next room, then the sound of shuffling papers.

'Here you are.'

With trembling hands, Bonnie took the newspaper. It was awful. Full view on the front cover, lying unconscious in a hospital bed with tubes coming from her mouth and nose. Bandages covered most of her legs and arms, but looking closer, Bonnie could see burned, blistered skin. When she could finally speak her voice came out in a hushed whisper.

'That's disgusting. I looked disgusting.'

'That's how it was, Bonnie.'

It was true and she could hear the pain in her mother's words. The hardest thing to bear was that everyone had seen this. Everyone knew that Bonnie Blake had lain helpless in a hospital bed, covered in ugly burns with skin peeling off. The invincible, cheerful Bonnie had been completely helpless. Bonnie let out a moan. 'How can I go back to school now? No wonder Belinda hasn't come!'

Mrs Blake sat beside her and pulled her close. 'You're healing, Bonnie. You're not like that now.'

When Bonnie didn't respond, Mrs Blake began to rock her and stroke her hair the way she had done when Bonnie was a little girl. Even her hair had changed. The lack of sun had darkened it and the once thick and healthy hair had become extremely thin. The doctors assured them it was a result of trauma and the hair would return, but it seemed to be taking a long time.

'I was a complete mess,' Bonnie muttered, still staring at the picture of herself.

'Yes, but we all are in some ways.'

'No, not me, Mum. Not before.' There was deep sadness in Bonnie's tone and her mother laughed gently.

'Maybe things seemed perfect in comparison with how you feel now, but it never would have lasted. Nobody's perfect. Everyone is in the process of ageing. Wrinkles form, hair changes colour, bodies wear out.'

Bonnie shook her head, refusing to be comforted. 'It happened too early.' She burst into tears and buried her head in her mother's arms. If only the world were a perfect place. If only decay never took place. Why did bodies have to wear out and die? There had to be more to all of this. Had to be more to life …

* * *

The knock at the door came for the third time and Bonnie forced herself to move her eyes away from the television. Slowly she made her way to the door. Blaze stood there, smiling.

She didn't return his smile. Why was he here? Had he finally gathered up the courage to face her again? Or had her mother told him she needed visitors? Maybe he was here because he pitied her. He seemed cheerful, but was there fear hiding behind those dark eyes? Did he dread looking at her the way she dreaded facing herself in the mirror each morning?

Blaze held out his hand to her. 'I brought something to show you.'

'You did?'

'Yes, but you'll have to come to the back fence with me.'

Bonnie flushed with embarrassment. It shamed her to think she was too weak to even walk that far, but it was the truth. All that training for the athletics carnival had been a complete waste of time. One accident and all her strength and fitness had disintegrated as fast as her 'perfection' had. She couldn't even walk to the back fence!

She took a deep breath. 'Sorry, I can't.'

Blaze's face fell and for a moment the old Bonnie returned. A sparkle of mischief came to her listless eyes, returning their old life. 'It's not that I don't want to see it. It's just a bit more romantic to be too weak to walk. You'll have to carry me. That's if you're up to the challenge …'

This time Blaze didn't blush and it filled Bonnie's heart with dread. Her presence had changed its effect on him now that she was no longer confident and beautiful. Everything had turned a full, horrible circle. Never again would she hear him call her 'Miss Perfect' and never again would he look at her with that awed, admiring expression. He was glancing over her thin, shapeless form.

'I could carry you. Will you let me?'

Once she would never have even considered it an option. But feeling disheartened and helpless, she merely nodded. He reached down, one arm going about her waist, the other beneath her knees. Then in one effortless move he lifted her. Her cheek rested against his shirt which held the familiar smell of horse. Her arms came up around his neck for support and she didn't dare look at him, but instead, shut her eyes tight. How could she look into his magnetic eyes ever again? How would he respect her after this? He walked in silence and then stopped. She felt his arms loosen as he lowered her to the ground, waiting for her to open her eyes. Finally she did and tried not to let out a scream of fright. There before her stood the largest horse she had ever seen.

'Peter Pan,' Blaze introduced triumphantly.

Bonnie's breath caught in her throat, her eyes widened in terror and she stepped back. Her whole body stiffened as she closed her eyes for a moment, the blood draining from her face. Her breaths began to come in short gasps.

Blaze was back at her side in an instant, his expression anxious. 'Are you okay?'

Bonnie stood completely still, unable to bring herself to move any closer to the horse. Her heart was beating way too fast. For a moment she couldn't answer for the dizziness that passed over her.

'Bonnie? What's wrong?'

He looked as scared as she was. She knew what was wrong, but she couldn't bring herself to speak. Pain. It was all too real, all too vivid in her memory. Images of a terrified horse dancing wildly through the flames flashed through her mind as she gazed in awe at Peter Pan. Her legs prickled with the sensation of heat and she could hardly breathe. Peter Pan truly was a magnificent creature, but she would have to admire from a distance. She took another step back and managed to make her mouth work.

'I'm tired. Can we go back to the house?'

Blaze studied her then shrugged helplessly as he came to lift her back into his arms. Bonnie closed her eyes, her mind replaying the night of the fire. Blaze's steady pace suddenly slowed and he stopped. Bonnie's eyes opened in surprise to meet sad eyes looking down into hers.

'Bonnie, what is it? What's changed you so drastically?'

She couldn't answer for the lump in her throat. Her eyes closed again and she felt Blaze resume his steady pace back to the house. She didn't open her eyes again until he lowered her onto the lounge.

'I need to sleep. Thanks for showing me your horse.' Her eyes slid shut once more before she heard Blaze mutter goodbye and leave.

Chapter Fifteen

Friends sent Bonnie flowers and cards, but only the Clements family and the local church minister visited her in person. Bonnie was terrified of returning to school but bore her fear silently. Glad it was winter, she pulled her school clothes over the compression garment she would need to wear for at least another nine months. She studied her face in the mirror. Only a few marks remained on her neck and the doctors assured her they would disappear completely within a few weeks. The compression suit would reduce some of the scarring on her legs and arms, but many of the marks were there to stay. She pulled on her gloves.

'Don't take them off. Don't take them off.' If she could remember that she should be fine. Fine? That's if she could every truly be fine again.

With a wildly beating heart she allowed her mother to drive her to the school gate. The principal met her with a large smile of greeting.

'We've missed you, Bonnie Blake! Even Miss Sanders has missed you in class, although you were hardly in there for long, anyway. And poor Brad hasn't had anyone to hassle. He's been totally lost without you.'

Bonnie chuckled with him and some of her fears faded. Things were still the same.

'You've missed quite a bit of work, but we've no doubt you will catch up quickly. We knew that if anyone could survive this you could.'

Bonnie smiled gratefully. It was going to be okay.

'Bonnie!' her friend, Sarah May, cried in delight as she entered the room.

'Welcome back!' Many people echoed the greeting, but Bonnie didn't miss the way they gazed at her curiously, some staring outright while others gave sideways glances whenever they thought she wasn't looking. Only Sarah May and Belinda treated her as they always had. Grateful for them, she turned to Belinda with a smile.

'So how's the debating team going?'

'Excellent. We've won every debate. I talked Blaze Clements into filling in for you. He's brilliant!'

Bonnie nodded, pretending she knew Blaze was debating but struggling with confusion. Blaze had never responded to her own pleading, so what had changed his mind?

As class began, Bonnie tried to concentrate. The teacher was speaking constantly and putting notes on the board. None of it made sense to Bonnie. The more she tried to piece together each word and sentence, the more it went over her head.

'I have to catch up on everything I've missed,' she told herself sternly. But the more she tried, the fuzzier her brain became. She looked out the window. There in the paddock beside the school oval stood Regal Zion. The horse standing peacefully by the fence brought such a flood of memories and images that it was all she could do to stifle a gasp. Class time blurred into recess when she was finally set free. Out in the open air her head began to clear and the stifling panic she felt in the class room was forgotten.

'How are you going, Bon?' Sarah May asked. 'Where are

those bright, laughing blue eyes we've been missing so much?'

Bonnie attempted a smile. 'They'll be back. I just need time to get back into the swing of things.'

Sarah May nodded and Bonnie knew her friend didn't know what else to say. She wished she could be her old self again, constantly laughing, teasing, unaffected by any adversity; so uninhibited and free. But she now knew what life really was, a struggle to survive and overcome pain, a fight to find hope and purpose. Just being alive wasn't enough anymore.

She heard a young male voice around the corner. 'Where's Frankenstein?'

'Frankenstein?' a female voice questioned.

'You know, scar legs.'

'Oh, her. I don't know. Probably sitting with her friends.'

The words passed over Bonnie without meaning until a year eight year old boy stood before her.

'Principal wants to see you.' It was the same voice she had heard only moments before. He had been talking about her? She was Frankenstein? Even the girl had known who he meant. Horrified, she stared at him.

'Now?' Her voice came out hoarse and raspy, the way it had ever since the fire.

'Yes, now. Or can't you walk that far anymore?' His eyes were cold and his words heartless. Once Bonnie Blake would have come up with a response that would have silenced him and made everyone laugh. Today she just sat feeling sick to the stomach and looking like an injured, frightened animal. Sarah May jumped up and grabbed the boy's arm, digging her nails in.

'You are so cruel!' She would have continued, but Belinda had now grabbed the boy's other arm and was throwing a torrent of abuse at him. Swearing began, going back and forth until a crowd of interested students gathered. Moments later, the deputy principal stepped in.

'What's this about?'

Nobody noticed the horrified Bonnie slip around the corner and out of sight but still within hearing.

Sarah May was shaking with anger. 'He was horrible to your niece!' Tears began to slide down her usually serene face.

'What happened?'

'He called her ... well, he just rubbed her accident into her face.'

Mr Richardson smiled. 'Bonnie's tough. She can look after herself. Now break this up.' With that he walked away while Sarah May and Belinda stared at one another.

'She can't cope,' Sarah May's face was contorted in her distress. 'Did you see her face? She couldn't take it.'

'I know,' Belinda agreed, her own face pinched with strain. 'Bonnie has changed.'

Bonnie took in a deep breath and headed to the principal's office. Yes, she had changed. Everything had. It was as though she were another person living inside this burned, scarred body. The old Bonnie had burned right along with that stable in the fire.

The principal was speaking to her; something about giving herself permission to take it easy, support available for her, care and concern from all the staff. And pity. It was there in his eyes.

It was an emotionally drained and discouraged teenager that Mrs Blake collected from school that afternoon. Tired and pale, Bonnie sank with relief into the passenger seat of the car.

'How was school?'

'Different.' Bonnie looked out the window at the hills and trees racing past. 'I used to love running home.'

'You will again someday.'

'Not for a long time.'

'You will get strong again, Bonnie.'

Bonnie looked down at her thin, shapeless body. Maybe she would, but life would never be the same again. Now that she was Frankenstein.

All night that name plagued her mind. Constantly the haunted faces of confused and uncomfortable friends played havoc with attempts to sleep. When she finally fell asleep she dreamed there was a fire in her room and she was trapped and then a large horse bolted straight toward her. With a shout, she awoke, drenched with sweat. Fumbling for the light switch, she took in deep breaths. She had to get over this. This constant torment was too much to bear. Light flooded the room and she heaved a sigh of relief. But then she looked down and saw those burn scars across her hands. There was no escaping the truth; she could never escape her own body. All she could do was be herself to the best of her ability, the way she had always done in the past. But her greatest fear still remained. What if her best wasn't good enough anymore?

Determined not to give in, Bonnie put on a brave face and returned to school. She would not allow people's reactions to affect her any longer. She would walk in that gate with her head held high.

'Scar-legs!' a year seven boy called out and gave a harsh laugh. Bonnie kept walking, pretending she hadn't heard. Another group of students stopped their game of handball as she walked past and whispered amongst themselves, watching her every move. One of them gave a little giggle.

'Ignore them. People are cruel.' Sarah May was by Bonnie's side, her face filled with pity. Behind her was Belinda who took a threatening step toward the group. 'If they say one more thing, I'll shut them up!'

Bonnie looked from one to the other. How she hated to be pitied! And how she hated anyone feeling they needed to protect her. When would this nightmare end? She wished she didn't have to see anyone, face anyone. If only she could be alone and not have to deal with all these people and their emotions and reactions to her. Then came the final straw.

Blaze strode toward her and his deep voice was filled with concern. 'Bonnie, I was watching out for you yesterday but didn't see you. How was your first day?'

Suddenly Bonnie had an urge to run; an urge stronger than she had ever felt before. But this time it was not for pleasure, this time it was flight! Glancing wildly around at the faces watching her with curiosity rather than friendliness, she threw her bag on her shoulder and ran. She was no longer fast and no longer was it effortless, but fear drove her on and anger gave her strength.

Gasping for breath, she headed out the gate and down the street. Running as if death was chasing her, she pushed her weary body. She felt she had been running forever, but she was only two blocks down the road, when Blaze caught her arm.

'Bonnie! Bonnie, stop!'

She didn't want to, but she was breathing so hard her chest hurt. She struggled to go on, wrenched her arm from his and struck out at him. He caught her hand and held her still. Too weak to fight any more, she broke into helpless sobs and fell wearily against him. At first he patted her shoulder cautiously, but then his arms came about her and he held her tight against his chest. When her cries subsided and her aching body stopped shaking, he released her and picked up the bag from where it had fallen on the ground. He took her arm with gentle determination.

'I'll walk you home.'

She stared at him, unwilling to admit she was too tired to take another step. He studied her a moment before understanding came.

'Stay here. I'll go and get Peter Pan.'

Bonnie watched as he jogged back to where the Clements'

horses stood eating grass in the paddock beside the school. What could she do? She was too tired to walk home but she was also terrified of the horse. She had to get a hold of herself. She had to. She fixed her eyes on Blaze as he effortlessly jumped onto the horse's back and headed her way. The closer he came, the more tense she became. By the time he and Peter Pan were by her side, she was shaking again, dizziness overwhelming her.

Blaze jumped down. 'I'll give you a lift up.'

He took her by the waist and easily hoisted her on to the huge creature. For a moment she panicked, but in one smooth motion, Blaze had landed back on the horse and sat himself firmly behind her. Bonnie knew he could feel how tense she was. One of his arms held her strongly in place and the other guided the horse. She tried to relax, glad Peter Pan was moving so slowly. Sighing, she collapsed against Blaze, unable to hold herself erect any longer.

'You okay?' Blaze's voice sounded deeper than usual with her ear against his chest. She nodded, her mind elsewhere, her heart heavy. So this is how it was to be helpless and out of control. She hated it. She hated life.

Chapter Sixteen

Blaze walked Bonnie into the house and explained what had happened to the concerned Mrs Blake. Bonnie didn't intend to stay and listen, but she couldn't help overhearing some of the conversation as she headed to her room.

'She's so different, now!' Blaze's voice was taut. 'I've never met anyone who loved life as much as she did. But now it's like she didn't really survive that fire – it took her life.'

Mrs Blake's voice was reassuring. 'Don't forget that deep inside she's still the same person, Blaze. She will heal. Just give her time.' Bonnie blocked her ears, unwilling to hear anymore.

* * *

For over an hour, Bill Richardson had been trying to persuade his niece to return to school. He admitted he hadn't taken Sarah May's words too seriously until other students gave details of the names she had been called and how she had run like an injured animal from the scene. He cringed now as she threw her scarred hand toward him.

'Look at it, Uncle Bill. It's disgusting. I have enough trouble living with it, so why should I make them? I'm visual pollution.'

'Bonnie –'

'It's true, Uncle Bill. My body has let me down totally.'

Uncle Bill laid a gentle hand on the fiery scars racing up her arm.

'This body is only temporary anyway, Bonnie. It won't last forever. These marks won't last forever.'

'That's right.' Bonnie's father had been leaning against the door frame, listening. Now he came to her and reached for her other hand. 'This body has only been given to us for our life on earth. It's what's inside that counts.'

Bonnie turned on her father, her tone accusing. 'I thought you didn't believe in God! You're talking as if there is an after-life.'

Her father lowered his eyes. 'I've changed what I believe. Your mother, Uncle Bill and I started going to church after your accident.'

'What?' Bonnie couldn't believe what she was hearing. 'How can you just change what you believe like that?'

No one seemed to know what to say until Uncle Bill gently released her hand. 'Sometimes trauma makes people start to think about what really matters.' He tucked a strand of hair behind her ear. 'Until your accident we had no reason to think about death or appearance … none of those concerns affected us.'

Her throat grew tight. 'Until now.'

'Yes, until now. But this could be a good thing. Physical decay can wake the soul.'

Bonnie said nothing, but her uncle's words plagued her mind constantly from that moment. Had her soul really been asleep because life was too comfortable? Was there more? If there was, how could she have missed it so completely?

Alone in her room that night, Bonnie called out to God. 'God, if you're up there, then please show me. I need to know.'

Even as Bonnie spoke to God for the first time, she knew a measure of fear. Yes, she wanted to know the truth, but if God was real, she had ignored him for a long time.

'Here I am talking to you when I don't even know you exist.' She shook her head. 'But I must think you do or I wouldn't be doing this, would I?' She let out a hollow chuckle, wondering if her prayer was irreverent.

'Sorry if I'm not showing you enough respect, God, but this is my first prayer, and well, I didn't really even know about prayer until I met Blaze.' Slowly she smiled. Somehow there had been relief in talking to someone supposedly in control. When life was such a mess she needed to know it wasn't all chance and that someone had it all in hand.

* * *

Bonnie didn't return to school. After several days of waiting at home and wondering if Blaze would visit, Bonnie wandered down to the back fence and looked out toward the charred remains of the stables and caravans. To her surprise, a waft of smoke rose into the air. Was Blaze there? Hadn't the Clements family moved into a house? Curiosity and yearning to see Blaze finally defied her fear. Taking a deep breath, she made her way across the paddocks. As she approached the smouldering campfire, the smell of smoke threatened to overwhelm her. She forced herself to keep walking toward the group sitting around the fire. It was them. They looked up expectantly, waiting for her to reach them.

'It's unreasonable, just a crazy phobia!' she reasoned with herself. 'Keep calm!'

All the memories were crowding in, and her heart was beating so fast she wanted to scream.

'Hey, Bonnie!' Starre greeted and the sound of her voice calmed the terrified teenager standing before them. 'Good to see you again!'

'Bonnie, we're glad you came!' Misty agreed cheerfully as

she tripped on the log she had been sitting on. 'We're just kind of saying goodbye to this place. It's going to be sold.'

Smiling, Bonnie looked around at them all. How fake her smile felt! Her heart sank as she realised Blaze was nowhere to be seen.

'I'm glad I came too,' she lied, avoiding looking in the direction of the burned stables. She met Storm's sneering expression.

'Haven't seen you at school lately. Everyone's saying stuff about you.'

'Shut up, Storm!' Starre snapped at him and Bonnie felt herself beginning to shake. Storm had always hated anything weak, Bonnie realised, and here he was staring at her scars, her helpless fear and timidity. She had never come under his hatred or scorn before. Now she was completely weak and his eyes were clearly saying he no longer respected her or cared.

The group sat in uncomfortable silence for a while and once more Bonnie felt the need to run; to escape their pitying, sympathetic looks and somehow be the person she used to be.

'Blaze's gone to get Shelley,' Misty dimpled, answering Bonnie's unasked question. 'She's coming to stay for a few days. Blaze is dying for her to meet you, so you'll have to come to visit us in our new house.'

So Shelley was coming. Shelley who bought Blaze his horse, who believed as he did and who converted him to Christianity.

'We thought we'd toast marshmallows around the fire for the last time tonight.' Prince gave her his charming smile. 'Want to join us?'

She shook her head. That was the last thing she wanted. To be with this handsome young man and know she was completely blemished. To have Storm sneering at her weakness and Misty oblivious to the whole thing. To have Beauty trying to overcome her guilt and Blaze talking with his beloved Shelley. And worst of all, to be standing beside the awful, crackling flames of the campfire.

Chapter Seventeen

The following day, Bonnie stood at the door of the Clements' new brick house with the large horse paddock beside. At a glance she knew it was perfect for the horse-oriented family. Peering in through the screen door she studied the girl on the lounge beside Blaze. Both turned at once to see her and Blaze jumped to his feet.

'Bonnie! I want you to meet my friend, Shelley!'

Shelley's smile was angelic and Bonnie's heart sank. She was everything she had expected, and more.

'Bonnie, I've been longing to meet you! I've been praying for you!'

Once, Bonnie would have told her bluntly that there was no need to pray for her, but now she stood silently with nothing to say. She smiled a half-hearted smile at Shelley. Why did she feel she was a threat to her own friendship with Blaze? Shelley was neither tall nor slim, as Bonnie was. In fact she was quite small and stocky. But all Bonnie could now see was that her skin was perfectly soft and pure. No scars. There was sweetness and peace radiating from her, along with a quiet confidence. Bonnie knew she could trust her completely, but she didn't want to trust her. She wanted to dislike her.

Shelley immediately took a genuine interest in Bonnie and her complete selflessness took Bonnie off guard. She didn't want to answer all Shelley's questions because it reminded her just how much her life had changed. She didn't want Shelley to care the way she did.

'What do you want to do when you finish school?' Bonnie cut in, trying to take the focus from herself and turn it back to Shelley.

Shelley smiled her disarming smile. 'I've applied for Bible college. There's a few that take students straight from high school.'

'What will that train you for?'

Shelley shrugged. 'Some kind of missionary or children's work, maybe. I'm not totally sure. It will teach me more about God, though. That's the main reason I want to go.' She turned to Blaze. 'Blaze and I looked into all the colleges in Australia and decided on the same one. It will give him the training he needs to be a minister, but it's got courses in children's work that I'm interested in, too.'

Blaze gave Shelley such an understanding smile that Bonnie's heart constricted. There was never such connection between Blaze and herself. He shared a bond with Shelley that she, as an unbeliever, could never have.

As Shelley chatted, Bonnie's eyes wandered around the room. She was pleased the Clements family had moved. Now she could visit without fear of fire and without seeing the charred remains of the stables. Hearing voices outside, she saw the rest of the family arriving home, riding gear in their arms.

'I love this land!' Misty was saying as she juggled horse equipment, finally dropping all of it.

'It's better than Collagg's Waterfall,' Prince agreed, 'All the rocks on that land made the riding so … oh, hello Bonnie!'

All five looked to where Bonnie sat on the lounge.

'What do you think of the house?' Misty bubbled. 'Has Blaze

shown you around?'

'Not yet.'

Starre lowered her saddle to the floor. 'Want to come riding with us tomorrow? There's some great hills on our land.'

'No thanks.'

'You don't have to ride one of the big horses. You could start with Penny Drop.'

Bonnie thought of the little pony-like horse. No, she couldn't even stand the thought of riding her. As she raised her eyes to refuse, she caught Storm's look of reproach and disgust.

'Don't push her, Starre. She's obviously too scared.'

Starre fell silent while Bonnie held Storm's gaze and took a deep breath. 'I'll come riding,' she said, 'but I don't want to ride the little pony-horse.'

Starre and Misty smiled. This sounded like the old Bonnie they remembered.

Chapter Eighteen

Bonnie stood looking at the horse, knowing she had to overcome her fear, and quickly. The Clements family would be here within five minutes and she needed Storm to see her riding that horse. Peter Pan – her own choice of name for a horse – so beautiful and yet so large and frightening. She remembered how she had once loved Victorian Dream's energy and wilful ways. Now she felt no affection toward these powerful creatures, but she had to prove she was still carefree, crazy Bonnie.

He wasn't saddled, but she couldn't do much about that. She didn't have time. It was an effort to climb onto the large creature and she couldn't do it without climbing onto the fence and then on to his back. She dug her heels in, taking a deep breath and trying to ignore her fear. As soon as Peter Pan began to move, she knew this idea had been a mistake. He was so strong and fast – she had no control whatsoever. He seemed to move faster and faster and she struggled, unable to think how to bring him to a stop. Her body was tossed from side to side as she clung on for dear life. She held on with all the strength she could muster and finally, with a mixture of relief and dismay, heard a shout from behind. Blaze was racing to catch up on Victorian Dream. She heard him call to Peter Pan, and then encourage her to hold tight. In a few moments he was at her side and had pulled Peter Pan to a stop. Bonnie sat breathing hard, her face all too easily displaying her shock and fear.

'What are you trying to prove?' Blaze's face was contorted with anger as he climbed up behind her. Roughly, he put his arms around her and moved Peter Pan forward, letting Victorian Dream wander back toward home on her own.

Bonnie shrugged and let her shoulders slump in defeat.

'I was just proving I'm still … well, I had to prove to everyone that I still can …' she stopped trying to explain and felt the tears coming. 'I failed,' she finally said as a sob caught in her throat.

'Only your own test – which was stupid anyway.'

She bit her lip, trying to stop her tears. Blaze was usually so caring and understanding but now he was angry, and that anger was directed at her. Nothing would ever be right again.

She felt the coolness in his silence as he helped her down and turned to his family who were waiting by the gate. Without so much as another glance at Bonnie, he explained what had happened in a strained voice. Bonnie dared to look around at them. Starre refused to look at her, while Prince and Johnny's expressions held such pity it made her feel sick. Misty seemed at a loss as to how to respond and Storm looked angry.

'Idiot,' Storm spat at her. 'You've got no common sense, Lady Lightning.'

That name no longer held respect or friendliness. Bonnie heard the sarcasm and disgust seeping through every syllable and she had had enough. Without another thought she ran home and this time Blaze just stood watching her go.

Bonnie stumbled into the house and sobbed into her father's arms. 'Please Dad, can we move? Can we go somewhere so I can start again? I can't take their pity anymore. I can't take the way Storm hates me and Starre won't talk to me. And Blaze is so angry with me. I can't concentrate at school because they're there.'

Bonnie's father held her for as long as she needed to be held, and then called his wife over. Bonnie hadn't noticed her watching in concern from the doorway.

'Your mum and I have already decided we should move.'

Bonnie's sobs stopped short as she stared incredulously at her parents. They had already decided?

Her father answered her unasked question. 'You'll be needing more skin grafts and it would be convenient to be near the hospital in the city. I've put in for a transfer with work and I was accepted today. I think it will be good for us all to get away for a bit.'

* * *

'Aren't you going to say goodbye to the Clements family?'

Uncle Bill was paying his last visit to the Blake home before they moved to the city. As deputy principal of the school, he brought many well-wishes from the staff and some of the students. However, none came to say goodbye in person and that was the way Bonnie wanted it.

Bonnie couldn't look at him. Instead, she allowed her eyes to wander the boxes packed across the floor. This empty house wasn't home anymore. But then, it hadn't felt like home since the fire, anyway.

'No. I haven't seen them all for ages anyway. No reason to make a big deal of it.'

'What about Blaze? He's been worried about you. He asks after you every day.'

'You say goodbye for me.' Day and night she remembered Blaze's strained anger after the incident with Peter Pan. He hadn't been to visit and Bonnie knew the friendship was over. He had his gentle, sweet Shelley now. He didn't need a confused, scarred girl to interfere with that relationship, and she was too proud to allow herself to be an inconvenience.

So, without a word to any of the Clements, the Blake family packed up their home of ten years and headed away from Everdeen. The new home was in the city, but Bonnie didn't care. Her love of the wide, open spaces had died with her confidence and freedom. Gone were the days when she could enjoy running across open paddocks, feeling the wind in her hair.

'I won't be able to run for a long time,' she told herself as they wove in and out of traffic. It was just too hot to run in the compression suit – and even if she took it off she needed to wear long sleeves to hide her burns and protect the sensitive skin from the sun.

The new home was nowhere near as large as the brick building that had been home in Everdeen, but for Bonnie it was perfect. In amongst so many houses and so much traffic she could hide very well.

Chapter Nineteen

Bonnie headed into the cool morning air with Copper by her side, watching each breath form a cloudy fog. Copper seemed keen to move faster and she found her own body longing to run again to escape the cold. Her body felt strange without the compression suit she had worn for so long and she was missing its warmth.

She held Copper back. 'Don't go too fast, boy.' He moved in beside her with his easy gait. As they jogged steadily through the park Bonnie saw the girl who walked her Labrador every morning. Her easy smile met Bonnie's again, but today she didn't continue past. She stood and waited to meet her. Surprised, Bonnie stopped and brought Copper to her side as he strained at his lead.

'I've been wondering for months what kind of dog you have,' the girl said pleasantly. 'Is it a spaniel?'

'No, an Irish Setter – he does have spaniel ears, though, doesn't he?'

The girl nodded, and her wispy blond ponytail bounced. She was pretty, Bonnie thought. There was something very open and friendly about her. Bonnie took a step forward and the girl fell into step beside her. 'I missed seeing you last week. You never usually miss a morning.'

Bonnie nodded. 'I try not to, but I was in hospital having surgery.'

It was clear the girl wanted to ask more, but restrained herself. Bonnie filled in the awkward silence. 'Going for a walk gives Copper his exercise and prepares me for work.'

'Where do you work?'

Normally Bonnie wouldn't have encouraged talk with a stranger, but seeing this girl's smiling face every morning had created an easy familiarity. Her youthful energy and friendly confidence reminded Bonnie of her own nature before the accident. Bonnie decided she could make a good friend.

'I volunteer at the Ashton Road Boarding Kennels. What about you?'

The girl laughed. 'Just school. Eighteen months to go and I'll be free!'

Bonnie nodded. 'I know what you mean. It can seem like a prison sometimes.'

The girl looked at Bonnie with open curiosity, and then held out her free hand for her to shake. 'I'm Emma Mathison. I live just round the corner in Ayleward Street.'

'And I'm Bonnie Blake. I live in Darby Street.'

She saw the way Emma looked at the burn scars on her extended hand but didn't comment as she shook it.

'Funny, isn't it,' Emma said with a laugh that set her blond pony-tail bouncing. 'It's been months that I've been walking past you in this park and wishing I had the courage to introduce myself. Then this morning I finally decided to just take a deep breath and do it and it's been easy as anything!'

Bonnie smiled and Emma shrugged. 'Well, I'd love to talk more, but I better head home and get ready for school. Catch you tomorrow!'

As Bonnie watched her go, she was aware for the first time

that she was lonely. Slowly she made her way home, ignoring Copper's insistent pull on the lead and deep in thought. Where was she going with life? True, she was extremely busy with the work at the kennels, but perhaps it was time to make some plans and gain some direction.

'Mum,' Bonnie called through the house as she hung Copper's lead on the door handle and let the door bang shut behind her.

'In the lounge room.'

Bonnie came into the room where her mother sat drinking her morning cup of coffee.

'Want some? The kettle's still hot.'

'No thanks,' she hesitated and her mother looked at her questioningly. 'Mum, I think I'm ready to go back to school.'

Mrs Blake's expression was thoughtful. 'You are?' She began to smile. 'What made you decide?'

'Just been thinking.'

Her mother nodded. 'I've been praying that you would want to – in the right time, of course. You have ability that shouldn't be wasted.'

Bonnie no longer cringed at her mother's mention of prayer. Both her parents had announced their conversion to Christianity not long after her accident. They didn't pressure Bonnie to go to church with them and neither did they pressure her to believe as they did. She couldn't help thinking that Blaze could have learned some useful hints about how to share his faith, from her parents. But then, Blaze was a teenager – merely a boy, really. He didn't have the maturity to know how to gain respect by living out life quietly, rather than debating and reasoning. Bonnie quickly changed her thoughts. Blaze had not entered her thoughts for a long time, and she wasn't going to allow the memory of him to bother her this morning. Today was a day to move forward and start living again. She was tired of merely existing. The doctors were finally happy with her progress and believed no further skin grafts or surgery would be necessary. It was time to move on.

Chapter Twenty

To her delight, Bonnie was accepted into the school Emma Mathison attended. They formed a fast friendship, and after being shown around, Bonnie settled into her first class. It was good to sit beside Emma and know she already had a friend.

'I'm really back to my old self!' she thought with relief as she listened with keen interest to the English teacher explaining genre. He made it sound so easy and she had heard it all before. He finished his explanation and then came toward her, carrying a spare text book. 'You might need to do a bit of catch up work, Bonnie.'

He sounded so apologetic Bonnie felt like laughing. She doubted she would need to do any catching up, but he would find that out soon enough. He might have trouble keeping up with her bright, inquisitive mind, and in the end might wish she weren't as academically proficient as she truly was. Her blue eyes met his and she knew he was waiting for her response. She gave a carefree shrug. 'That's fine. I won't find it a hassle.'

He smiled. 'I thought not. Here, you need to sign for the text book.'

She took the pen from him and signed. This was a new beginning. The old Bonnie was back, but she was in the damaged Bonnie's skin.

'Hey look!' Emma reached across and pointed to the name a few lines above where Bonnie had signed. 'My brother had this text book, too.'

Bonnie looked. Aaron Mathison.

'He's a lawyer. Hmm, maybe you'll end up being a lawyer too.'

Bonnie sputtered out a laugh. 'What? Is there something special about this particular text book? Does it have magic powers that make you want to debate and argue everything? Or does it make you an expert on deception?'

Emma giggled. 'You think that's what lawyers do?'

Bonnie pulled a face. 'Hmm, as your brother is a lawyer, I would like to retract that last statement on the grounds I might incriminate myself.'

Emma chuckled. She shared most of Bonnie's classes and did a good job preparing her for each. Physical Education was next and as Emma packed her English books into her bag she gave Bonnie a rundown.

'PE is one of those subjects everyone loves or hates in this school. Our teacher is nice enough, but she really favours anyone with natural talent. Those students are treated like royalty. But the rest ... well, they end up feeling like complete failures because they are just not one of those lucky ones. Believe me, I speak from personal experience.'

'What, experience at being royalty?'

'You've got to be kidding! I'm talking about the other end. The clumsy, complete failure end.'

Bonnie was surprised. 'Even after walking your dog every morning?'

Emma chuckled. 'You wouldn't even ask that if you saw the way I groan and carry on as I force myself to get up every morning.'

Bonnie grinned, wondering how her fitness compared with

that of the others in her class. She definitely wasn't as fit as she once had been, but she had regained a lot of strength in the last year. She certainly couldn't be deemed unfit!

Mrs Elton gave such a welcoming smile Bonnie wondered just how much Emma had exaggerated.

'Bonnie, I'll need to do a fitness check on you.' She glanced around at the class. 'The rest of you start your stretches and I'll get Bonnie ready for a timed lap around the oval.' Bonnie was aware of the curious glances from the students around her. Not pitying or haunted; just as curious about the new girl as she was about them.

'You might want to take off your track pants and wear shorts,' Mrs Elton suggested. 'It's warming up out there.'

The other students were moving to begin their stretches as instructed. What should she do? She could make a scene by refusing to change her long clothing or she could let them all see who she really was under it all. She couldn't afford to think too hard about it. She just needed to do it. Her burn scars looked much better, and these students didn't look like they were immature enough to make up hurtful names and insults. Shorts and t-shirt it would be.

'Are you ready?'

Bonnie nodded and stood poised at the starting line.

'Go!'

As Bonnie ran, the students gazed after her, noting the speed of the well-shaped legs which tore around the track with graceful style. And Bonnie knew then that the burns were not insurmountable. The students could clearly see them, but they were insignificant to a class and teacher so focused on talent and speed.

Emma met her at the finish line with her friend, Laura. 'You're fast! How'd you learn to run like that?'

'A new favourite to add to the list,' Laura agreed, chuckling as she pointed to Mrs Elton. The teacher stood transfixed. Then as though woken from a daze, began jotting down times, nodding her head in approval as she did so.

'Bonnie, I'd like you to join our athletics team.'

Bonnie nodded as she gasped for breath. It had been a while since she had pushed herself so hard.

'You've obviously run before. How much experience have you had?'

'I was involved with school athletics for years but I've had a break for a while.'

'Hmm, it shows. You've got great style. You realise that if you join our team it's going to take a lot of commitment?'

Bonnie nodded. 'That's okay. I'd like to do it.'

'From your parents, too. We have before and after school training. They'll need to be willing to drive you.'

Bonnie grinned. 'Actually, I can drive. I have my licence.'

Mrs Elton's surprise changed to a smile. 'Perfect.'

Bonnie saw the way the other students looked at her in awe. Most of them weren't old enough to have a licence and clearly thought it was something special that she did. For the first time she felt her last two years hadn't been wasted. Learning to drive had been a good use of her time.

* * *

Bonnie watched Emma as she rummaged through her school bag for her drink bottle. She couldn't help liking the girl's confident, gentle nature. Emma was the type of girl you could ask anything and she would answer with that same gentle, open smile. And there was something different about her. Bonnie wanted to know more.

Emma suddenly let out a cry of triumph and held up her drink bottle.

'Got it. I must have like, this secret passage somewhere in my school bag that it escapes down. It goes into a totally different world and then returns in its own time. If only it could talk. The adventures it must have!'

Bonnie laughed at her. 'Well, with your imagination I'm sure you could tell me all about them.'

'My imagination? Bonnie, you have no idea. My head is a completely different world. Aaron, my brother, is always telling me I'm on another planet. But then, when it comes to real life I'm as normal as they come.'

Bonnie grinned. 'I'm sure that's not true. What do you do in your spare time? I bet you search for new worlds in your wardrobe.'

'Sorry to disappoint you, but I just walk the dog, do a bit of sewing … and,' Emma averted her eyes seeming awkward for a moment, 'prepare for Sunday School. I teach the kids.'

'Sunday School, as in church?'

'Yeah.'

'You're a Christian?'

Emma's awkwardness faded at Bonnie's open look and the light in her eyes gave the answer. 'Yes. Are you?'

'No, but my parents are.'

Emma nodded, taking in the knowledge with calm acceptance. 'Have you ever been to youth group?'

'No.'

'Would you like to? My brother runs one for our church. We have games and supper and a talk about God. And once a month we have an outing where we go bowling or something. All sorts of people come, whether they believe or not. It just gives them a chance to hear about God without feeling threatened. We don't expect any response or anything like that.'

Bonnie listened in amazement to Emma's simple, honest

explanation. Where did this girl learn to share her faith in such a comfortable, easy way?

'I'd love to come, but I might be too old. I missed quite a bit of school and I'm back here as a mature aged student.'

Emma nodded. 'Yeah, I figured that. But you're only a couple of years older, aren't you? We have some uni students that come along, so you'll fit in okay.'

So it was arranged. Bonnie would go ten pin bowling with the youth group that Friday night and she would pick up Emma on the way.

Chapter Twenty One

'Hey, Emma!' Laura called out with a grin as Emma and Bonnie came in the front door of the bowling alley. 'Managed to drag another unsuspecting victim into your religious trap, have you?'

Emma gave a good natured laugh and turned to Bonnie.

'Laura's not a believer, either.'

'She's not?' Bonnie chuckled. 'So should I be worried that Laura considers this a trap?'

'Nah … Laura's paranoid about everything.'

Laura heard, just as Emma had intended. She gave her friend a playful slap before running off to join a group of guys standing around the pool table. Bonnie let her eyes wander the noisy and crowded bowling hall. She was nervous but she wasn't going to let them know that. She wanted to appear controlled and together – like the old Bonnie would have been.

A young man was watching them from one of the bowling lanes. His eyes fastened on Emma.

'Hey, Em! I've got some spare places here if you and your friend want to join me.'

Emma gave him an engaging smile and a nod. She leaned over to whisper in Bonnie's ear.

'That's Carl. He was in Year Twelve last year and now he's an apprentice mechanic.'

It was clear Carl was very interested in Emma. He cheerfully asked Bonnie about herself and introduced her to all his friends, but the whole time his gaze kept returning to Emma. There was such tenderness in his expression Bonnie felt like an intruder just witnessing it.

Emma giggled her way through the games, falling, sliding, dropping and having a great time. Her giggles stopped when Carl came to her side to help her direct the ball down the alley. Bonnie smiled at the blush she saw on her friends' cheeks. And through her mind flashed a picture of Blaze. Just as quickly she pushed it away. She was here to make a new life for herself; to have fun. The group played game after game and Bonnie thoroughly enjoyed herself. The atmosphere was light-hearted as the group teased, laughed and competed. They had almost finished their third game when a voice came over the microphone.

'Time to pack up, guys – return your shoes, say goodnight and head home.'

Bonnie stopped mid-bowl to look up at the counter and see who owned the cheerful voice. Who was he? He was fair-haired and she was sure she hadn't seen him before. So why was there something so familiar about him? She turned back to complete the bowl. She'd work it out later. As the group slid off their shoes to return them to the desk, the familiar looking young man from the counter approached Emma.

'Are you coming home with me?'

Emma scowled at him. 'Nope. Mum said Bonnie can drive me.'

He glanced at Bonnie then back to Emma. 'You sure she's responsible?'

Emma's annoyed look only caused his face to break into a cheeky grin. Bonnie stepped in before Emma could voice her clearly uncharitable thoughts.

'I've had my licence a year now.'

'No worries. I was just teasing.' He held out a hand for her to shake. 'And since Emma hasn't bothered to introduce me, I'm Aaron, her big brother. I lead this youth group.'

There was a hint of pride in his voice. Bonnie shook his hand and smiled, now realising why he looked so familiar. His fair complexion and fine features were very much like Emma's.

'I'm Bonnie Blake.'

'I deduced that. I haven't heard anything but your name for the past few weeks … apart from hearing about Carl, of course.'

With that, Emma sent a horrified glance in Carl's direction and hit her brother with the shoe she had just taken off.

'Aaron! He's right behind us!'

Aaron grinned without remorse. 'Wouldn't you prefer he accidentally found out you are keen on him so he can make the first move? I'm doing you a favour.'

Emma swiped at him with the shoe again but he moved out of the way. With a quick wave to Bonnie he moved on to speak to another group.

Emma talked as Bonnie drove her home. 'Aaron took over leading the youth group once Dad got too busy to do it anymore. Since he's finished uni and become a lawyer he thinks he's better than everyone else. He gets a bit big for his boots sometimes.'

Bonnie said nothing, thinking that Aaron seemed big brotherly rather than arrogant.

'I have to admit he's a good study group leader, though. I guess he gets that gift from Dad.'

Bonnie swung the car around the corner into Emma's street. 'Study group?'

'Yeah. The believers in the youth group meet every Wednesday night for a Bible study.'

Bonnie wondered if Blaze had ever had the opportunity to

learn so much about the Bible with other young people. It was a pity he always had to read text books. She had to get Blaze Clements from her mind. She glanced from the road to Emma with a teasing look.

'So you discriminate against non-believers, hey?'

'Well, yeah, I guess we do,' Emma responded, the same teasing in her tone. 'You can always pretend to believe so you can join, though.'

'No, I might get caught out. That would be just way too embarrassing.'

Emma laughed, then said goodnight as they arrived outside her home. Bonnie turned the corner to her own home, unable to erase Aaron's smiling face from her memory. Life was improving every day.

* * *

Bonnie settled comfortably into school life and enjoyed the new friendships she formed. She was living again. Truly living. Youth group became the highlight of each week and she believed she had found a place in this new world she inhabited. The noise and activity of the city drowned out any unwanted thoughts. And she was even coming to terms with living in a body marred by burns, so long as she could keep out any memories of Blaze and his God. Yet, she knew she couldn't hide forever. Emma was very transparent and every time she tried to surreptitiously study the scars, Bonnie knew the time for questions would come. It did.

They were studying together for their semester English exam. Bonnie had thought she was ready but the question still took her completely by surprise. Maybe she had expected Emma to slowly draw her out, or hint in a subtle roundabout way. Instead she just looked directly at Bonnie and came out with it.

'What happened to your hands and arms?'

She stalled by pretending to mark her place in her English notes and slowly look up to meet Emma's curious gaze. 'I got burned in a stable fire.'

'Did you own horses?'

'No, they belonged to some friends. One was trapped in the building and I tried to save it and got badly burned in the process.'

Emma's sympathetic eyes were wide now. 'Did you save the horse?'

'Yes.'

She didn't quite snap the answer, but it gave Emma the hint. Bonnie didn't want to talk about it and wouldn't. It was in the past and would stay that way as long as she could help it.

Emma smoothly changed the subject. 'Laura reckons she's never seen anyone run as fast as you.'

Bonnie smiled with relief that Emma had let it go. 'She hasn't seen many people run, then. I might have the style, but I haven't got the speed back yet.'

'You used to be faster?'

Bonnie nodded, not liking the way the conversation threatened to return to the past. 'We'd better get back to study.'

Emma nodded and turned back to her textbook. Bonnie breathed a quiet sigh of relief and returned her mind to exams.

The exams took up a lot of time, but Bonnie enjoyed every moment of them. She had always enjoyed the satisfaction of collecting knowledge from her bright mind and filling in the blank exam paper. And exams took her memories down different paths away from the fire.

Emma and Laura were much more excited to see the end of the exams. Laura waved as she headed toward the school gate. 'See you two tomorrow! I'm going out to enjoy my freedom.'

'Just make sure you do it legally.'

Bonnie and Laura laughed at Emma's admonition, but Bonnie wondered at Emma's confidence. She was so open about her beliefs and standards, but always managed to present them in a nice way. She looked up to see Mr Rush coming their way. His eyes met with hers.

'Can I see you for a moment in my office?'

'Me?' Bonnie couldn't imagine why he would want to see her, but followed him, giving Emma a wave as she left. Mr Rush offered Bonnie a chair, then sat down at his desk. She was relieved that he came straight to the point.

'Bonnie, you have been nominated by several people to be school captain next year. I need to know if you're willing to accept the nomination.'

She stared at him, speechless. Her as captain? Why? Mr Rush took her silence as consent and continued.

'It will be a big commitment, but I believe you can do it. You will need to write a speech and present it when –'

'No, no I don't want to accept,' Bonnie cut him off, finding her voice. 'I'm just a bit surprised. Why would anyone nominate me? I haven't been here that long. What are they thinking?'

Mr Rush studied her as though not sure whether to take her seriously. At her completely blank look his expression changed and he began to smile.

'Maybe you're just a bit likeable? It's hard not to respond to someone who is fun-loving and down to earth, don't you think?'

'And responsible,' she added with a cheeky grin. 'I like to think I'm responsible and trustworthy, too.'

He nodded. 'Yeah, that too. How about it?'

'No thanks.' She didn't even need to think about it. 'I don't think I'm school captain material.'

Mr Rush seemed taken aback by her quick rejection of the idea. He fiddled with a paper clip on his desk, then met her eyes, his words slow and careful. 'Why not let the students decide that? Others have been nominated, too, including your friend, Emma. The students will decide after all the speeches have been presented. You have time to think it over. The speeches aren't till first week next year, but we'll be printing the voting forms in about two weeks.'

'No, I don't need to think it over. Thank you anyway.' With that she stood and left the office, her mind trying to sort through what she had just heard. Who on earth would nominate her for school captain, and why? Her cheerful, friendly nature had helped her make friends quickly and easily, but she hadn't thought she had made enough of an impact for anyone to consider her for such a position.

'I haven't even topped any classes,' she muttered as she returned to class. 'I'm not a high achiever anymore. What have I got to offer?'

* * *

Life became hectic for Bonnie, but that was how she liked it. Filled with constant sporting and academic commitments, she had less time to think, and the less she thought, the less she hurt. She passed Year Eleven with flying colours, although couldn't manage to top Emma's near perfect marks. And despite her growing speed and fitness in physical education, the school athletics champion managed to outdo her easily.

'It's different in the city,' she told her parents with a tired smile once the year of study was finally over. 'More competition and more work with fewer results.'

Mr Blake smiled back. 'You don't call these results?' He held up her report card. 'For someone who vowed they were never going back to school, I'm pretty happy with these.'

Bonnie took the report card from his hands and glanced

over it again. The results were pleasing. For the first time in her life the teachers hadn't written the comments Mr and Mrs Blake had become familiar with:

'Bonnie is bright but distracts other students.'

'Bonnie has done well but tends to talk too much in class.'

'Bonnie's positive results fail to reflect her disruptive nature.'

She grinned as she remembered Miss Sander's comments. It was rather hard to complain about a student who topped the class even though she only spent half the year inside, the other half out in the corridor. Thankfully, she had matured in the last few years and was ready to really work. And tonight she was finishing it all off by attending the end of year youth group event. A few games in the church hall would be the perfect end to a good year.

However, as she arrived at the church that evening she was directed to the church building itself, rather than the hall. It was clear that Aaron had planned something different altogether. She hadn't been to church in years and she didn't like the feeling. It was crowded and unfamiliar. Rows of chairs were lined up facing the stage, and the stage was filled with musical instruments.

Feeling uncomfortable, she found herself a seat in the back row. It wasn't long before Emma and Laura joined her. Aaron was coming to the microphone and Bonnie frowned as she leaned over to speak into Emma's ear. 'What's going on?'

Emma waited for Aaron to ask everyone to be seated and then turned to Bonnie with a shrug. 'I think he's got some guest speakers in.'

'Guest speakers? What kind of speakers?'

Emma didn't answer as Aaron's voice came over the microphone again to introduce the band now standing on the stage.

'This is Matt, John and Clive. They're here tonight to teach us a few songs. Some of you may know them already, so feel free to sing along.'

Bonnie frowned as the words to a song were placed up on a screen. It was lively enough, but the words made no sense to her. It was all obscure – something about seeing God. She knew that was a physical impossibility. Even Blaze had admitted God only spoke in a person's heart or through the Bible.

As the night continued in a similar fashion, Bonnie's discomfort changed to anger. No one had warned her she was going to be placed in such an unfamiliar environment. Hadn't Emma said these youth group events were aimed at non-believers and not meant to be threatening? Well, she felt threatened! And Aaron looked so smug. He was looking around at the members of the youth group listening spellbound to the guest speaker, Sandra Thorne. Sandra had just three months to live. It was as though Aaron thought that was enough to convert the group. His eyes met hers and she glared back. She was not hanging on Sandra's every word. In fact, she was planning her escape. In the next moment, escape is exactly what she did. It was hard to gather belongings with anger fuelling every movement and even Sandra looked Bonnie's way as she wrapped up her talk. Emma reached for her arm, disappointment written across her face.

'You're leaving?'

Bonnie glared at her. Emma had probably expected her to fall into a sobbing heap and give her life to God, too. The thought made her fume and her answer came back in barely a whisper. 'I didn't come here to listen to some woman's sob story!'

A few people turned to look as she stood and abruptly left the hall. She saw Aaron trying to move casually through the crowds toward her and she quickened her steps. With relief, she moved out into the darkness of the night. Funny how darkness could be a relief after overwhelming brightness. Light and noise could smother faster than anything. Like flames hissing and lapping …

'Bonnie!'

She jumped at Aaron's voice behind her and turned to face him. He was breathing hard and she wanted to slap him for chasing after her. He should have left her alone!

'What's wrong?'

He looked genuinely concerned, but she closed her heart and stepped back to put distance between them. 'I hate emotional manipulation, that's what!'

She began to walk away, but he fell into step beside her. 'Tell me about it.'

Her laugh was harsh and sarcastic. 'What? Pour out my own sob story to you? Will that make you feel better? Or will you not be able to claim victory until I actually convert to Christianity?'

'Bonnie –'

She spun to face him. 'You didn't tell us there would be no games tonight. First you hype us up with some lively songs, then abruptly change to soft, heart rending music before a woman comes on to tell how she's dying of cancer and then as her dying wish begs us to become Christians. It's pathetic! It makes me sick!'

'Perhaps you're angry because you've been challenged?'

His gentle reply fanned her fury. 'No, I am not challenged! If anything, this will turn me off Christianity. If I ever decide to search for the truth, I want to do it without emotional hype and without feeling manipulated. I want down-to-earth facts. If Christianity can't cater for real life, then why bother with it?'

With that, she turned and stalked away. To her surprise, Aaron reached out and grabbed her arm. She struggled, but his hold was firm.

'You're too smart for your own good sometimes, Bonnie Blake.'

There was no gentleness in his voice now. He was angry, too. His hand was tight around her sensitive burns.

'No, Aaron. You are. Do you honestly think that performance tonight will reach the parts of my heart that are hurting? Are you so arrogant you think you understand what's going on inside me? Only God knows that. If He really cares and if He really knows everything, why don't you leave the converting to Him? He doesn't need your help – or interference or whatever it is.'

Her bright eyes burned into his and this time it was he who turned and walked away. Bonnie was left rubbing the spot on her arm where his fingers had been.

Chapter Twenty Two

Emma and Bonnie still spent a lot of time together at school, but Bonnie no longer went to the Mathisons' home and she refused to discuss any topic related to God. Though Emma had to have noticed the change, she didn't comment. Bonnie thought the issue was safely settled until Emma approached her in the school library. The fact that she had left it to the very last minute on the very last day of school spoke volumes. This was not something Emma had wanted to do. Her usually serene expression was fraught with tension.

'Um, Bonnie, Aaron wants me to ask you to come to the last youth group outing for the year.'

'He does?' Bonnie didn't plan to help Emma do the asking. It was clearly Aaron's idea. She couldn't imagine him feeling bad about the last event so he must still hold out hope of converting her.

'Yes. It's tonight. So will you come?'

'I thought Sandra's night was the last one.' Bonnie didn't even look up from the paper she was punching holes in. 'Didn't Aaron convert as many people as he wanted to?' She placed the paper in her folder and shut it with a snap. Finally she looked up to see Emma's hurt expression. Maybe she had been a bit harsh but she honestly wasn't interested in risking another youth group.

'It's going to be a Christmas party at the roller skating rink.' Emma tried to reassure her. 'No talks or anything like that.'

'No,' she began, then saw the hope in Emma's eyes. It wasn't Emma's fault she had a brother like Aaron. Emma had been nothing but genuine and respectful when it came to discussions on God. She had never pushed and had always been honest and open. 'Okay, I'll come. But only because you'll be there – not because your manipulative brother asked me!'

Emma grinned at the description of Aaron, then her eyes lit up. 'Reece Downham is coming, too.'

'Reece? Who's Reece?'

Emma looked surprised for a moment, then laughed. 'Where have you been the last few weeks? Reece is the new guy at school.'

'That tall one with glasses?'

'Yeah. You've met him?'

'I think so.'

Bonnie tried to remain casual. Reece had actually paid a lot of attention to her, although she hadn't asked his name. At times she had been uncomfortable with the way he smiled at her and always seemed to be looking in her direction. It now seemed she would have to avoid Reece Downham at all costs while she was anywhere near Emma. It appeared that Emma might have feelings for him.

However, avoiding Reece at the roller skating rink was a lot harder than she thought it would be. It was only twenty minutes into the evening and Reece was looking her way again. Bonnie wished Emma would accept Carl's offer to roller skate. She was tired of constantly inching away from Reece to avoid hurting Emma's feelings. He was heading over and Bonnie tried to back away without looking like she was avoiding him. She hadn't skated before, so it was a little awkward to move gracefully in the skates which seemed to roll in every direction but the way she wanted.

'Hey, careful!' A laughing voice came in her ear as strong arms stopped her from tripping. She turned to look into Aaron's cheerful face. He was grinning at her.

'What are you trying to do? Avoid one man just to bowl over another?'

Bonnie stared, unable to comprehend his meaning. His smile grew wider.

'I've been watching you. That poor guy is going to end up exhausted chasing after you if you don't slow down.'

Bonnie felt her face redden. 'Sh!' she hushed him. 'That's Reece. Emma likes him.'

'Oh, I see – that's the handsome Reece I've heard about all week. Quick, you'd better skate with me for a while.'

With that he took her arm and led her into the rink. She was grateful his hold was more gentle than it had been the other night. It was firm but held none of the force that had both hurt and scared her last time. Tonight she had on long sleeves to protect her burns.

'I can't skate, you know,' Bonnie warned, but he shrugged and smiled.

'You don't need to be able to when your partner knows how.'

Bonnie allowed herself to be led around the rink. Aaron guided her smoothly and gave instructions as they went.

'Let your feet roll outways a little bit, then push and lift.' She almost lost her balance and Aaron laughed. 'Take control of the skates – don't allow them to control you.'

Bonnie did so and soon found herself skating quite well. Aaron nodded in approval.

'You picked it up quickly.'

Bonnie glanced back, trying to spot Reece, and almost slipped. Aaron grabbed her arm firmly and righted her.

'Let me do the spying. You just skate and look like you and I are committed.' His eyes moved down to the scars on her hand. 'Emma tells me you were burned in a fire.'

'Yeah. What's Reece doing now?'

Aaron gave her a knowing look but allowed the diversion. 'I think we've convinced him. He's talking to Emma.'

'Excellent! You can take me back now.'

Aaron studied her for a moment and she saw he was amused. 'You expect me to take you back just because you command it?'

'Oh, I get it.' Bonnie threw him a wry smile. 'Now is when you start trying to convince me to become a Christian. Is this how you've achieved all your conversions?'

She had spoken without thought, but Aaron didn't appear offended. Instead he met her eyes with an honest, frank expression.

'You mean God's conversions? No, it doesn't work to get people on the defensive.' He turned his skates to face her and took both her hands in his. 'If you push too hard people end up avoiding you completely and you don't even get to have a friendship anymore. I learned that the hard way.'

So he regretted it. The knowledge surprised her. Before she could respond he had let go of her hands and led her back toward the outside of the rink. He settled her onto a seat and was about to go when she touched his arm. 'What do you mean by God's conversions?'

Aaron lowered himself to the seat beside her. 'I don't believe I can convert anyone. Only God has the power to change hearts and lives. That was my mistake with the last youth group. I wanted to do it myself, my own way. I'm sorry I upset you.'

She frowned, totally taken aback by his apology. 'You don't

have to worry about not being able to convert me.'

He raised an eyebrow.

'I think God's been working on me for a long time now. And I think He does use people; He uses Christians to make people who aren't Christians think a bit deeper about Him.' She gave a sudden grin. 'Even when we don't want to think about it.'

'Is that right?' Aaron's eyes were bright with interest. 'Could it be possible that self-sufficient Bonnie Blake is actually beginning to believe?'

'I don't really know.' She turned distractedly to where Emma and Reece were now making their way into the rink. 'I'm right on my own now. Go and help some other helpless maiden.'

She jarred at her own words. How could she say that to Aaron? Despite sharing Blaze's faith, they were nothing alike. It was years since she had teased Blaze about rescuing a poor, helpless maiden. Only she had been the maiden. Never would she allow Aaron to rescue her. As for Blaze, he'd had to do it one too many times.

* * *

Uncle Bill came for Christmas. Bonnie was delighted to see him and raced out to throw her arms around him. 'I've missed you so much!'

'Likewise!' He returned her fierce hug, then stepped back to study her. 'You're looking so well. It seems the old Bonnie is back!'

Bonnie merely smiled as she picked up one of his bags to carry inside. In some ways he was right. In others she would never be the same again, but she would not let him see that if she could help it.

'I have all sorts of news to tell you and messages to pass on,' Uncle Bill informed her as he followed with his suitcase. 'Some of your old friends miss you almost as much as I do.'

A picture of Blaze flashed through Bonnie's mind and she almost tripped.

Uncle Bill looked concerned. 'You right?'

Bonnie nodded and turned her face away. Her uncle stood looking at her, a thoughtful expression on his face for a few moments before he started back toward the house. Bonnie knew then she would have to do a better job at hiding her emotions. She refused to let Uncle Bill know how much she still hurt – how much she had to work to force away memories just so she could survive. Maybe it was not so good he had come to visit after all.

Chapter Twenty Three

Bonnie had been talking non-stop. It was easier to talk about her own life than to let Uncle Bill speak about his. Because his life was the one she used to be a part of, the one she had needed to leave behind just so she could survive. She caught her breath, about to begin again, but Uncle Bill took advantage of the pause.

'Belinda said to say hello and to tell you the debating team did you proud and used obscure words no one knew the meaning of.'

Bonnie simply nodded, searching her mind for a change of subject. She couldn't come up with one quickly enough and Uncle Bill kept going.

'Starre Clements was the national champion – can you believe that? Quiet Starre. She was hiding her talents from us. She happens to be – '

'They don't have debating up here.'

Uncle Bill nodded, but ignored her attempt to keep the topic away from Everdeen. His expression had sobered. 'We've had some sadness in the town. Do you remember Rachel Seton?'

Bonnie nodded, her heart beating a little harder as she remember the talented pianist who had been in her class.

'Her parents were killed doing mission work overseas.

Rachel seems to be coping very well, though. Her faith has carried her through and she's more mature than she ever was.'

Rachel's parents? Mr Seton had been the church minister who had come all the way to the city and visited her in hospital while she had been in a coma. He had been the one who provided support for her family during the ordeal. She pushed it from her mind, not wanting to think about it.

When Bonnie said nothing, her Uncle took a deep breath. 'But that's not all, Bonnie.' The way he paused made her pay attention this time. There was something different – something serious and sorrowful in his tone. She waited. He swallowed hard, his eyes filled with regret.

'Blaze Clements has tetanus.'

The words hit hard like a physical blow. She gasped, then pulled herself together. To her own surprise her voice came out calm, almost detached. 'Tetanus? How'd he manage to get that?'

'His horse. He had a cut that got infected.'

She nodded. Uncle Bill came to sit directly beside her. He took both her arms and turned her to face him. He waited until her eyes met his.

'Bonnie, he's fighting for his life.'

Bonnie felt a wall of protection come up between her and the news. It was as though she was dreaming what Uncle Bill was saying. Her nightmares about Blaze were common enough. This was just another one and she needed to shut it out just like she did all the others. So she merely nodded then jumped up as she glanced at her watch.

'Wow, I'm late! I have to go. Sorry, Uncle Bill, we'll have to catch up later.' With that she rushed from the house and jogged all the way to Emma's place. Maybe it was rude to leave Uncle Bill like that, but she couldn't sit there with him a moment longer. Why did he insist on telling her so much? She had left the life of

Everdeen behind and she wanted it to stay in her past. But Blaze … tetanus? No, it didn't sit right. She felt devoid of any emotion as she wrestled Emma for the black bean bag. She won as usual and settled back to face her.

'How does a person with tetanus die?'

'I'm not sure.' Emma turned to Aaron who sat watching cricket on television. 'Aaron?'

Aaron turned from the television for a moment. 'I think their muscles become all tense and they have fits and become delirious. I've heard it's pretty awful. Why?'

Bonnie shrugged. 'Just wondered.' She forced a casual grin toward Emma. 'So how's Carl taking your new friendship with Reece?'

Emma's face became downcast. 'I'm so confused, Bonnie. I think Reece likes you, really, and I still kind of like Carl. How do I know who I'm in love with?'

Aaron let out a laugh at his sister's problem while Bonnie jumped up and tried to tip him off the chair he sat on. 'Get out of here if you're not going to be sympathetic.'

Still laughing, he got up to leave. 'You'll be sorry. I'm the only one with the answer to Emma's teenage woes and you're throwing me out.'

Emma glared at him and he disappeared just after he was hit by a flying bean bag.

It was late when Bonnie arrived home, but Uncle Bill was still up. The look he gave her was serious.

'Bonnie, we need to talk.'

'What's up?'

'You didn't give me a chance to finish telling you about Blaze.'

'Uncle Bill, I'm tired …'

'Bonnie, will you talk to me without running off or interrupting please?'

Bonnie saw the pleading look in his eyes and slowly sat down. 'Blaze might die, Bonnie.'

When Bonnie said nothing, he reached for her hand. 'I think you should go and see him, to say goodbye.'

It was said so bluntly but gently that Bonnie felt a shock go through her. This was real. Blaze Clements really might die. As it sank in she sat in complete silence, seeming to stare at nothing. Then she looked at her uncle, pain clouding her eyes.

'He won't want to see me in his dying moments.'

'No, this is for you, Bonnie. He's delirious and probably won't recognise you, but you need to say goodbye.'

'I already said goodbye, Uncle Bill. In my heart I let him go. I just never gave him the chance to say goodbye to me.'

She was aware he watched her as she slowly made her way to bed. Why couldn't he just let her keep running? She'd been doing it so long she didn't know if she could stop if she tried.

* * *

Bonnie rushed toward the door first thing after breakfast. She needed to run.

Uncle Bill called to her from the kitchen. 'Where are you going, Bonnie?'

'I've got to train for athletics.'

'It's the middle of the holidays.'

'Yeah. We still have to keep fit if we don't want other people to get ahead.'

'Well, before you go, I just thought you'd like to know I've heard some more news from the Clements family.'

She nodded. 'It'll keep. I've got to go, Uncle Bill.'

But as she opened the door his firm grip on her arm stopped her. What was he doing? She looked up to see an expression on his face she had never seen before. It was determination mixed with pain.

'Bonnie, when are you going to stop running?'

'Running?'

'From the things you don't want to hear; the things you don't want to go through. You pretend to be so brave and strong, but you're a coward. You're so afraid, you can't stand up and face the real world. You run from every fight.'

Bonnie frowned, offended. 'Uncle Bill, I'm not running. I'm just busy.'

'Have you ever talked to anyone about what happened that day?'

She didn't need to ask. She knew exactly which day he meant. 'No, but I don't need to.'

It was clear that he did not believe her. 'You're not training for athletics this morning, Bonnie.' She stared at him in amazement. What right did he have to tell her what she could and couldn't do?

'I'm not going to let the school down, Uncle Bill.' She tried to leave, but he still held her arm.

'Dad?' Bonnie's eyes pleaded with her father who had just entered the room. He looked sad as he shook his head. 'Bonnie, I'm sorry. I should have made you work through the trauma earlier. Uncle Bill is right. You're running. We need to deal with this thing.'

Bonnie felt a tightness grow in her chest and her voice came out high pitched. 'Thing? What thing? There is no thing.'

Her father let out a deep sigh. 'You can miss one day of athletics, Bonnie.'

'And we're going to talk.' Uncle Bill firmly closed the door.

Helplessly, Bonnie looked around for an escape, but there was none. There was nothing to do but sit down. Her father sat beside her, her uncle directly across. She appreciated the comforting hand her father had on hers. He spoke first.

'What is it about the Clements family, Bonnie?'

'Nothing, Dad. Honestly, it's okay.'

'No, it's not okay. What is it?'

She glared, trying to work out what her father and uncle wanted from her. 'They're not part of my life anymore.' She didn't mean to snap but she was becoming angry. How dare they force her to talk about the past? It was private, her business, not theirs. 'Why is that so hard to accept?'

'Because you ran from them. Why? Blaze was your closest friend. What happened?'

'He got too religious. He made me uncomfortable.'

'Couldn't you have worked out your differences?'

'No, because his religion said I'm going to hell.'

'Well, if you didn't believe it, why should that bother you?'

'Because it made him so upset.'

They sat quietly in thought for a moment while Bonnie looked around the room, hoping this would all end soon and she could get out and go for a run. This was ridiculous, being held here and interrogated like a prisoner.

'What happened that night, Bonnie? What changed you so much?'

'Nothing. I told you. I've worked through it. I'm fine.'

'You're not fine.'

Bonnie threw her Uncle a stubborn look. 'You don't know my heart. I'm coping. Well, I was until I got sat down here like a child in trouble.'

She knew she was acting childish and probably deserved to be treated like a child in trouble, but she had to do whatever it took to get out of there. The walls were closing in, suffocating, trapping her like that burning stable.

Her father finally spoke. 'Bonnie, I don't want you involved in athletics for now. Not until you're able to talk about this. I think you need to slow down for a bit – leave yourself some room to face your fears.'

Bonnie turned from her father to her uncle in angry defiance. 'What have you been saying to him?'

Her father spoke before Uncle Bill could answer. 'Just what I needed to hear, Bonnie. You're running and you need to stop. There's so much we need to deal with. I know a lot of physical healing has taken place, but you still need emotional healing. We should have talked this through a long time ago.'

Bonnie went to her mother in frustration. 'What am I supposed to do?'

'Face your fears. See a counsellor like Uncle Bill suggested.'

'Face my fears? But Mum, it won't help anything. It will just prove I'm right to be afraid. This world is not a nice place, that's all there is to it.'

Mrs Blake wiped the angry tears that had sprung from her daughter's eyes. 'I never thought I'd see my Bonnie this way,' she whispered, and there was a tremor in her voice. 'You were always so … so carefree and strong, but for some reason God has willed this. Perhaps so we would see our need of Him.'

Silence seemed to invade the room as Bonnie's mind thought over those words. Her mother continued holding her close, but all Bonnie could hear were Blaze's words so long ago. He had prayed that she would see her need of God. But even Blaze had never wanted her to go through something like this. So why would his God want her to go through it? How could she believe that God really loved her now? And if God loved Blaze, too, why was Blaze dying? None of it made sense.

Chapter Twenty Four

The hospital building loomed large and frightening. That building represented pain to Bonnie. It represented permanent change. Life or death. It held so many memories they threatened to squeeze the life from her. She could hardly breathe, but her mother was right. It was time to face her fears; to face Blaze. Step by step she forced herself to move toward the main entrance. News had come from Uncle Bill that Blaze was improving, but no one could promise anything. Never had Bonnie felt such a turmoil of emotions – such anguish, yet such anticipation. She was going to see Blaze Clements again.

The nurse at the reception desk typed in Blaze's name and scanned her screen. 'Here we are. Blaze Clements has been transferred from Intensive Care to the ward just this morning.' She looked up and smiled. 'Well, that's good news, anyway. Are you family or friend?'

'Friend.'

'General visiting hours end in twenty minutes.' She glanced back to the computer screen. 'He's in five C East. If you take the lifts to level five you can follow the signs to the nurse's station from there.'

Bonnie nodded. She didn't need directions. She had been

in this hospital often enough she knew every corner of it. The burns ward had been her second home after the accident.

Memories of her time in hospital plagued her as she walked through the clean corridors and into the ward. She knew the pattern of the room numbers. She didn't need to speak to a nurse at the station – didn't want to speak to one. She just wanted to quietly make her way into Blaze's room and see for herself that he was alright. What she would do from there she had no idea. Five C. There it was. Taking a deep breath, she looked around the corner. And there sat Shelley. Her angelic face was gazing down at the form lying in the bed. What should she do? She couldn't see Blaze's face from where she stood, but Shelley was here. That made all the difference. This was not how she imagined it would be. The familiar, sun-browned hand resting on the sheets moved feebly and Bonnie saw the gauze taped over it. An IV line had been removed. Another good sign.

Shelley suddenly reached forward. 'Sky, don't touch that, darling.' A dark-haired toddler came into view. Shelley bent down to lift the little girl into her lap and that's when Bonnie noticed it. A gold diamond ring on Shelley's finger. Shelley and Blaze were engaged – perhaps even married? No, surely they were too young for that?

Footsteps came down the corridor and Bonnie stepped back from the door, pretending she was looking at the noticeboard outside. A doctor strode past and into the room. His face held a smile as he picked up Blaze's chart from the end of the bed. 'You're definitely on the mend now, Blaze.' He flipped it shut again. 'There's even talk about you going home.'

Shelley dissolved into tears of relief and Bonnie felt uncomfortable witnessing such emotion. She forced herself not to run. Then a weak voice, hoarse voice came from the bed. 'Don't cry.' Blaze's hand reached for Shelley's. 'It's good news, not bad!'

Shelley laughed through her tears while Bonnie wished she were game enough to walk in and see Blaze's face.

'You and Sky go home now,' the voice said to Shelley and he sounded weary and unlike the determined Blaze Bonnie had once known and loved.

The toddler came to the side of the bed and reached up. 'Uncle Blaze not sick now?' Her voice was tiny and frightened.

'No, Sky. I'm much better now. I'll be coming home soon, darling.'

Sky. The name rang a bell and Bonnie remembered. Blaze had been so angry when Prince ignored the fact that he had a daughter. Yes, Sky would be two now. Sky was Prince's daughter! Blaze said he wanted to take care of her. Now it seemed that he and Shelley were doing just that. Bonnie didn't need to hear or see any more. She had faced up to her fears and seeing Blaze face to face now would only cause deeper pain. Reality hurt. She turned away, a lump constricting her throat. So close but so far …

Her steps were heavy as she headed back out toward the nurses' station. She held herself back until she was past the entrance to the ward and then she ran. Wildly she looked around. She couldn't take the lifts. She needed freedom. Where were the steps? Why did they have to be in a different place on this floor? Finally she found the doorway to the stairs and yanked it open. She took the stairs two and a time and didn't stop running until she was out the door and standing in the sunshine. Panting, she looked back to the entrance of that awful building.

Her father was right, she realised with startling clarity. Uncle Bill was right. She was running. She was afraid. No longer did she run out of the pure pleasure of living. She was driven by an inner shadow that seemed to become larger and larger as the days went on. It gripped her heart in so many ways, but now one of her greatest fears had been realised. Blaze Clements was gone from her life. Not through death, but through loving someone else. Why couldn't she feel joy for him?

Tears streamed down her face as she sat in her car in the hospital car park. She felt so lost and alone.

'God, I can't live like this. But I can't stand this pain, either. If you're there and you care, then help me through this! I'm so tired of running and I don't think I have the strength to keep going.'

She banged a hand on the steering wheel. She didn't want to think, didn't want to face all this, but she had to. It was time. But then, maybe Blaze and Shelley weren't really engaged. Perhaps Shelley married Prince and they were looking after Sky? Even as she thought it, she knew it was not possible. Settling back in her seat, Bonnie decided it was time to accept reality. She, Bonnie Blake, was scarred, but not handicapped or disabled. She was still intelligent, even though life was not as easy as it had once been. She had a lot of good friends and so much to be thankful for. What about God?

She thought back to the book her mother read every morning along with the Bible. It was supposed to explain Bible passages, but the one Bonnie had glanced at simply hadn't made any sense. About the temporary 'tent' of the body or along those lines. The words came back to her now. It was true, this mass of skin and bones would not last. She had come face to face with that reality as the flames licked at her body in the stable two years ago. In brief moments of consciousness in those first hours in hospital after death had stared her in the face, she'd decided if hell was one continual, unconsuming fire like the one she had experienced that day, she would do anything … anything to ensure she didn't go there. She had often shuddered at the thought but forced it away deep inside her. But now …

'Okay, God. I want to find out the truth, because I'm scared of hell,' she admitted. 'I'm scared of you, too. Ignoring you didn't stop you interfering with my life. I know you do whatever you want to do and I can't stop you. I hate that I had no control in what happened in the fire. Blaze couldn't stop the fire either and he believes in you!'

She sighed deeply. 'So since you won't leave me alone. Since you did this to me, I want to find out why, and I want to find out how I can avoid letting you do anything like that again!'

With those words, Bonnie let her mind replay the past for the first time. It occurred to her as she did so that her heart didn't beat wildly and she didn't have the urge to run. Something about Blaze and Shelley being together finalised what she had once desired but now knew could never happen. It hurt, but at the same time she felt incredible peace because she was going to make sure God was in her future.

Chapter Twenty Five

Bonnie couldn't bring herself to go straight home. Dad and Uncle Bill would want to know how Blaze was and she wasn't ready to talk about it just yet. She headed to the Mathisons' home instead.

Aaron answered the door and smiled when he saw Bonnie. 'Haven't seen you for a while. How's things?'

Bonnie moved past him, unsure how to answer. She chose not to and instead settled herself in the lounge room.

'I've got a few questions I need answered, Aaron.'

He raised his eyebrows before lowering himself into the bean bag. 'Must be serious. You didn't fight me for the bean bag.'

Bonnie sighed. 'Yeah.' She glanced up as Emma came into the room.

'Bonnie! Where have you been?'

'Searching for answers. And that landed me back here.'

Emma sat down on the edge of a chair. 'What's going on? What do you need to know?'

Bonnie pointed down at her burned legs and arms. 'Why God allowed this. Why He won't leave me alone.'

She would have laughed at their shocked expressions had her questions not been so important. She saw the way Emma closed her eyes and knew her friend was praying for answers.

Aaron took the lead as usual. 'What do you mean God won't leave you alone?'

Bonnie shrugged. 'I hadn't even thought about God most of my life, then all at once it was like I couldn't get him out of my mind. I tried to ignore it because I didn't think I had any needs, but then the fire came and totally messed up my whole life. After that I had needs but nothing to offer God, either. I thought I had it all together, but I'm a complete mess.'

Aaron glanced at the burn marks on her body and then quickly away. Bonnie had noticed it before. Aaron struggled to even look at her burns. He swallowed hard before meeting her eyes again.

'How did the burns mess up your life?'

'Well, it changed my whole personality for a start.' Her eyes met his in a frank way. 'I lost all my confidence once I experienced real fear and pain. I just couldn't enjoy life anymore. It meant I couldn't run in the state athletics carnival I had been training for all year. I couldn't concentrate in classes anymore …'

'But Bonnie, you're good at sport and school.'

Emma looked confused and Bonnie wanted to laugh. Emma truly had no idea. 'Not like I used to be, Em.'

Emma picked at the edge of the lounge chair. 'I'm sure there's a good reason for the accident!'

'I hope so, but somehow I doubt it.'

'Why?'

'Because even my friend who tried to convince me to become a Christian started doubting his faith when this happened.'

Emma reached across for the bowl of chips on the coffee table, her expression thoughtful.

'Not even Christians fully understand God. Even Dad doesn't usually understand the way God works.' She threw a handful of chips in her mouth. It was then that Aaron stepped in. He stood and looked down at Bonnie.

'Had this guy who lost his faith been a Christian for long?'

'About a year, I think.'

He shrugged, his expression knowing. 'What can you expect? Emma's right. People who've been Christians for years still struggle to understand God and why he does some of the things He does.'

'What's the use, then?' Bonnie demanded, becoming angry.

It was then that Mr Mathison walked in. Emma let out an audible sigh of relief. 'Dad, Bonnie's got some questions we can't answer.'

'We have answered them,' Aaron contradicted. 'She just won't accept the answers.'

Mr Mathison looked from his son and daughter then back to Bonnie. His look was understanding as he reached a hand to her.

'Why don't you come into my office and speak with Mrs Mathison and me?'

Relieved, Bonnie allowed him to take her hand and pull her up. She wasn't getting much help from Aaron and Emma. Being a minister, surely Mr Mathison would have some answers?

Once settled in the office, Bonnie felt rather nervous.

'I just wanted to know why God let my accident happen.' She glanced from Mr Mathison to his wife. Neither seemed shocked by the question, but the whole set up in the study with the door shut and two people gazing at her made it all seem so serious.

'It *is* serious,' a voice inside her said. 'This is about life and death … eternity!'

With renewed determination, she straightened, looked directly at the couple and waited. Mrs Mathison spoke first, her steady gaze making Bonnie feel as though she could trust her.

'Well, Bonnie, I don't know that we can give you an answer, but that's what faith is all about. Knowing God enough to trust him with what you *don't* know.'

Bonnie frowned. This wasn't the direct answer she had been hoping for.

'That's right,' Mr Mathison agreed with his wife. 'God wants us to trust Him, even when we don't understand. That's what faith is all about.'

'So I shouldn't be demanding explanations from God, no matter how much I'd like to know?' Bonnie feared she would just have to accept that answer and resign herself to never really understanding.

Mr Mathison smiled. 'We can always ask. And I would dare to say I have a bit of an idea why God would allow something as awful as your accident.'

Bonnie's eyes lit up as hope filled her. 'You do?'

'Yes. I believe God allowed your accident because He loves you.'

Bonnie stared at him incredulously. 'What?'

'Well, did you ever question life or death before the accident?'

'Not really.'

'Did you recognise your body was only temporary and that your soul had needs?'

'No.'

'Did you recognise that you sin?'

Sin. That word Blaze had used that meant doing the wrong thing. Like lying. Like ignoring God and not living completely for Him.

'Not until I met a … a friend who's a Christian.'

'Sometimes Bonnie, a fatal illness shows no symptoms. God

used this accident to bring out the symptoms of a dying soul. All your restlessness, your depression, emptiness and fear were telling you something was wrong deep inside. Now you've recognised the symptoms, you can search for the doctor to heal you.'

Bonnie stared. How did he know how to describe her feelings so accurately?

'Who better to heal you than the God who made you and loves you?' Mr Mathison waved a hand toward the church building next door. 'It's what I've been saying every Sunday – that Jesus dying on your behalf was the way the Father created the cure. Now you have to accept it and use it.'

Bonnie frowned. He had started to make sense and then he brought in all the things she couldn't understand. About Jesus dying. It was a concept that never seemed real to her. She hated this feeling of confusion.

'Bonnie, imagine you were perfectly healthy again. Imagine all the rest of the people in the world had a disease and were dying. Then it was discovered that in your body was the cure – the one medical answer to everyone's survival. But gaining the cure to help everyone else would mean an operation that would kill you. Would you do it?'

Bonnie shrugged. 'I couldn't say unless it really happened, but I'd like to think I would.'

'What about your father. Would he allow it?'

Bonnie remembered her father's tear filled eyes as he sat by her hospital bedside. She liked to think of him as a hero who would do anything to save the world, but could he let his daughter die for that purpose? Bonnie didn't like the uncomfortable thoughts and gave Mr Mathison a defiant look.

'What are you getting at?'

'Jesus had the only cure for dying souls, Bonnie – the cure for the disease of sin we are all born with. His Father God asked him to give his life to save us. The cure is to have His Spirit living within us, but we have to ask for that to happen. God doesn't force the cure on us. It's our choice.'

Bonnie thought of the horrible fire she had been through. Jesus wanted to save her from having to go through that kind of torment eternally. And His God allowed Him to die because He loved her, because He wanted to spend eternity knowing her and having her know Him and love Him. For the first time she began to understand how much God loved her. Her previous fear of Him turned a full circle and with tears forming in the blue eyes that had been defiant only moments earlier, she looked into the faces before her.

'I believe,' she whispered. 'I don't want to have the disease of sin anymore.'

Mrs Mathison came around the other side of the desk and took Bonnie into her arms. She held her tight as she shed tears of her own.

'Oh Bonnie, I've been praying for you for so long. Your mother told me about your tragic accident the first time she came to our church.' She reached for her husband's hand. 'We began praying from that day. First, that you would all come to know God, and then that He would use this traumatic experience you've been through for His glory. This is a complete answer to our prayers!'

Bonnie looked from Mrs Mathison to Mr Mathison and gratitude filled her heart. Unable to help herself, she spoke out loud to God.

'God, I'm sorry that I've ignored you for so long. I'm sorry for believing I was okay spiritually and that I could live without you. I need you and I've finally stopped running. Please use your cure to heal my dying soul and help me get to know you. There's a lot I still don't understand, like about your Holy Spirit, but I trust you to give me the answers I need.'

The look the Mathisons gave one another showed their amazement at her depth of understanding. Bonnie embraced the peace that washed over her. It was cleansing and complete. She felt as though an empty space within her had finally been filled. She walked out of that room a changed person. Her beaming smile spoke volumes as she faced Emma and Aaron's questioning gaze.

'I believe, you guys, finally I believe. I've never known peace like this before, even before the accident.'

Emma's face lit up as she came and threw her arms around Bonnie. Aaron stood back looking more sceptical. Bonnie chuckled at him. 'It's okay, Aaron, I understand a bit of why. And the bits I don't understand I'm okay with. Before my accident I didn't know anything was missing because I'd never known pain. Without knowing pain, you can't appreciate joy. Without knowing you have needs, you can't appreciate the one who can fulfil those needs.'

She had to get home. Smiling, she imagined what would happen when she opened the front door and announced the good news to her parents.

Chapter Twenty Six

Bonnie knew she would never forget the expression on her parents' faces when she announced that she now believed as they did. It was as though time stopped still for a moment and settled in eternity. They stared at her in awed silence, but in that moment there was a connection, an understanding, a completeness in her relationship with them that she had never experienced before. It was as though she were no longer burned and scarred, trapped within her physical body. Something within, something much deeper, was complete and satisfied; set free.

As her parents hugged her tight, she remembered the time as a child she had sat with her father on the back step of their home, watching the sun sink over the hill. There had been a moment, a brief glance of time where she had known there was something more to life than she could ever understand; something deeper than she had ever experienced. Now she knew she had caught a glimpse of God that day. God had been speaking to her young heart, trying to catch her attention. Well, he had her attention now.

Her mother was the first to find her voice. 'You know, the angels in heaven are rejoicing right now!'

Bonnie grinned, enjoying the delight shining from her

mother's eyes. 'They are? Why?'

'Because another person has come to believe and fulfil their reason for existence.'

Bonnie just shook her head, finding it all too much to take in at that moment. 'I'll believe you.' She fell silent, remembering Blaze Clements' face as he had asked her what she was born for.

'The moment!' had been her response. How naive and blind she had been. For the first time she understood Blaze's frustration with her. Picturing his serious, dark eyes as he had tried to share the truth with her, she shook her head. It was too late now. Finally she believed, but Blaze had his beloved Shelley and it was too late. Glancing down at her burned hands, she remembered the anguish he had so clearly expressed in his voice and eyes when she had been burned. He could never love her, anyway. Not now that she was so burned and scarred. But she would meet him again in heaven, and that was what she would have to look forward to. No longer burned, she would smile at him and thank him for praying for her. There would be an eternal connection between them, no longer blemished by unbelief or physical decay. She couldn't wait for that day. She longed for it more than anything she had longed for in her life.

* * *

Bonnie glanced up to see Laura and Emma coming into the school library. She gave them a cheerful wave then went back to her game of cards. She was surrounded by younger students waiting for their turn to challenge her. Bonnie's blue eyes sparkled with amusement as she studied young Jake Lockett who had hidden a card up his sleeve. She looked under the table with exaggerated innocence. 'Now I wonder where that missing card could be?'

'Maybe it fell on the floor?'

Bonnie wasn't fooled by the suggestion. With quick reflexes she grabbed at Jake's arm. Jake jumped up, while Bonnie unsuccessfully attempted to force the card from him. It was no use. She would just have to give up.

'Need some help?'

Bonnie looked behind her to see who owned the voice. Reece. 'Yep, see what this young man here has up his sleeve. Literally.'

Reece obliged and sprang on the boy, wrestling him to the ground. The group laughed as the two struggled until Reece finally came up with the card. The commotion caught the attention of everybody else in the library and Bonnie cringed at the look that passed over Emma's face. Both Emma and Laura had commented on how much she had changed, but it wasn't clear whether Emma thought it was positive or not. At times Bonnie would catch that look passing over her face – it wasn't dislike entirely, but something close to it. It confused and worried Bonnie. Was it because Reece paid her so much attention?

Reece interrupted her thoughts as he handed her the card. 'Can I join in?'

She avoided his eyes, acutely aware that Emma was still watching. 'I don't know. You'll have to ask Jake.'

'Sure!' Jake called with a grin, 'but you're not allowed to win or you get kicked out of the game.'

Reece let out a laugh. 'I'll try not to.' His disappointment was obvious when Bonnie stood and left her place in the game.

She shrugged. 'I won, so I'd better leave.'

'No, don't go, I was just joking.' Jake pleaded, but Bonnie just smiled at him as she pushed in her chair.

'That will teach you to cheat and make up rules.' She gave them a cheerful wave and headed over to Emma and Laura. Laura gave a welcoming smile, but Emma's look was rather pointed.

'It's funny how you get along better with little boys than

the guys in our year, Bonnie.' She turned to Laura. 'Have you noticed that, Laura? She does, doesn't she?'

Bonnie grinned. 'That's because the younger boys are more interested in having fun than romance.'

'You got something against romance?' Laura asked in surprise.

'No. It just hasn't leapt into my path.'

Laura laughed. 'I think it has, Bonnie Blake. You just haven't noticed.'

Bonnie shook her head. 'Ever since I got burned everything has been different, including the way guys look at me. But that's okay, I'm not worried about it.'

Laura turned to Emma. 'Can you believe this girl? She's got everything going for her and she can't see it.'

Emma shrugged, not looking at Bonnie. 'She's got a nice personality.'

Her tone was so begrudging that Bonnie had to fight her hurt. She made herself laugh.

'I know that line, Emma. That's what people say about anyone who isn't attractive or talented. It's a last resort in finding something nice to say.'

Emma frowned. 'You know I didn't mean it that way.'

'Well, how did you mean it?'

'I don't know.' She flung a hand downward. 'You're so oversensitive these days!' With that, she stormed off, leaving Bonnie and Laura looking at one another. Laura put a comforting hand on Bonnie's shoulder.

'Don't worry about it. She's the oversensitive one these days. Anyone would think she doesn't like the change in you since you became a Christian. If it helps, I like it. It's good to see you so … well, alive and happy.'

Bonnie was grateful for the encouragement but she couldn't leave things the way they stood. She needed to understand. She needed to speak with Emma.

She arrived outside the Mathisons' door that evening to hear voices inside. She raised a hand to knock, and then stopped as her name was mentioned. It was Emma's voice and it sounded bitter.

'Bonnie just flirts all the time.'

'She does?' Aaron sounded surprised.

'Ever since she's become a Christian she's changed. I hope she didn't make a commitment just so Reece would have her.'

Bonnie frowned at the words, puzzling to understand Emma's purpose in slandering her.

'Emma, I think you're being a bit harsh.' That was Aaron's voice again, but Emma cut him off with a laugh that made Bonnie cringe.

'Don't tell me you've got feelings for her, too?'

'No I don't. For your information I don't find her at all attractive.'

'I don't believe you!'

'I don't.' Aaron's voice had become loud and indignant. 'For a start, I find her burns a bit repulsive. Secondly, she's got an arrogant independence that …'

Bonnie had heard enough. Deeply hurt, she turned and headed back out the gate. She had seen the way Aaron avoided looking at her burns and she could forgive him that. But he didn't like her as a person? He had attacked her character and that cut deep. What had she done to make him think she was arrogant? She had no idea.

'Bonnie, I've been hoping to catch up with you!'

Bonnie was jarred out of her thoughts. Reece was heading up the footpath toward the Mathisons' home. She couldn't avoid him this time. Perhaps it wasn't the right thing to do, anyway. She had danced around him for weeks now, for the sake of her best friend. But was Emma her friend at all? Bonnie simply didn't know what to think. Her joy of the past weeks had gone.

Reece looked concerned. 'Hey, what's up? You've lost your sparkle.'

She hesitated, wondering how much she should tell him. Could she trust him? Could she trust anybody? He looked at her with a concerned kindness that caught her off guard for a moment. She couldn't stop the tears that formed in her eyes.

'I just overheard something I wasn't meant to hear. Something I wish I didn't hear.'

Compassion clouded his eyes. 'Let's walk,' he suggested, and she followed him past the Mathisons' home. As they wandered along the path, he waited for her to speak. Finally, she did, disappointment and pain in her voice.

'I guess I just thought Christians were … well, meant to be better people than everyone else.' She wiped at a stray tear. 'I mean, I know we're human, but I'm just so disappointed.'

'In yourself or other Christians?'

'Both, I guess. I don't think I'm much good at being a Christian. All of a sudden I seem to be making mistakes and hurting people.'

Reece smiled. 'Or else you're noticing it for the first time. Knowing God has a way of showing us what we're really like.'

Bonnie pondered his words, then acknowledged he was right. She remembered with regret the way she had made Blaze so uncomfortable with her teasing and upset him with her carefree words. Now she had hurt Emma enough to cause her to be hurt in return.

'I was selfish,' she recognised. 'I *am* selfish.'

Reece nodded in agreement. 'We all are, but don't forget we are also forgiven if we ask to be.'

Bonnie felt her heart jump at his intense, serious look. She found it hard to remain calm when deep eyes so much like Blaze

Clements' were looking into her heart and mind. She wished she could look away, but she couldn't. She needed his wisdom and friendship right now.

He gave a gentle smile. 'I was really excited to hear about your commitment to Christ. It's been an encouragement to so many people.'

An awkward feeling filled her. How should she respond to the depth of feeling he was putting behind his words?

His smile deepened. 'Hang in there, Bonnie Blake. As you know, life is not a fairy tale and being a Christian doesn't solve your problems – it just gives you the strength to face them and know God has a purpose in it all.'

Bonnie felt warmed by his mellow, down-to-earth voice as he gave her encouragement and realised what she had been missing by avoiding him. He might have been younger, but he was definitely not immature.

'Thanks.' She gave him a smile, then also thanked God for sending him into her path to encourage her. They walked in comfortable silence until they reached her home.

Reece turned to look directly into her eyes, his expression filled with understanding. 'I'll keep praying for you.'

So she had been in his prayers for a while. The thought took some of the pain from her heart. She thanked him again then watched as he walked back down the footpath. He even walked a bit like Blaze, she thought. Strong, steady and sure. She shook her head in confusion. She simply couldn't let her thoughts go down that road. Not now. Not ever again.

Chapter Twenty Seven

Bonnie didn't know what to say when Emma invited her to come around and help prepare her school captain speech. It felt deceptive to pretend she didn't know what her friend truly thought of her. But maybe Emma was wanting to talk to her about it – to sort it all out. As much as she dreaded the thought she knew what she should do.

Emma gave her a confident smile and threw her the black bean bag. 'Here, I won't even fight you for it today.' She giggled. 'I have my speech almost finished but was hoping you could help me – I think it still needs a few touch ups.'

Bonnie hesitated. 'I'm not sure I'm the best person for that.'

'Of course you are! You're great with words.' She sobered. 'Though I have to admit I can't understand why you didn't accept nomination for school captain. Didn't you think anyone would vote for you?'

Bonnie shook her head. 'I was afraid they would and I would be deceiving them. I haven't achieved anything for this school, Emma. Thanks to you, I haven't even topped a class.'

Emma chuckled. 'Come on, I know you're not really upset about that. You haven't got a jealous bone in your body.'

Bonnie, however, couldn't smile. Emma seemed so friendly

today, but it was hard to forget the cutting remarks she had heard from the front door only days before. Were people really so double sided?

'Do you want to hear my speech?'

Bonnie didn't know how to answer. She suspected her opinion didn't really matter to Emma anyway. Being nominated for school captain had changed Emma somehow. She was more confident, but she was also a lot more interested in herself and her own achievements. She listened as Emma began reading out her list of achievements. They were impressive but just like her own past achievements they seemed empty.

* * *

It was the day for the speeches. Bonnie stood before the assembly, smiling as she spoke into the microphone. 'Welcome, everyone. I get to lead assembly today. Mr Rush reckons I need a taste of leading to see what I'm missing.' She grinned over at Mr Rush. 'Sorry, Sir, I've tasted but I don't really want to swallow.'

'Just get on with it, Bonnie.' He was smiling but she knew he meant it.

'Fine.' She gave a grin and a shrug that left the students laughing. 'Right, today we get to hear the speeches of our potential school captains. Laura Hazelhurst is now going to present her speech.'

Laura made her way to the front, visibly relaxing as she met Bonnie's friendly eyes and smile. Bonnie handed her the microphone, then sat back to listen.

'… In conclusion, I would be proud and honoured to be your school captain.' Laura finished after listing her achievements in the school. Bonnie had had no idea of the extent of them until that day. She had thought Emma's sounded impressive but she had nothing on Laura.

Next was Greg Lionel who had a similar list of achievements. His conclusion, however, was much stronger than Laura's. 'We need a strong, powerful leadership in this school,' he told the students, 'and I can fulfil that requirement. In representing this school I will bring it a good name and be a valuable asset to all students. It would be an honour to be your face to the public. Consider how you want this school to be viewed by outsiders. I am sure you will be as proud as I will be to have me as your figurehead.'

With that, he sat down while Bonnie tried to gather her thoughts. Was it arrogance or honesty these nominees were presenting? The next two speeches were very similar and Bonnie hoped Emma would outdo them by presenting something a little different. She said she had made changes – Bonnie hoped she had made a lot or she wouldn't stand out from the previous nominees at all. She handed over the microphone.

'And finally, Emma Mathison.'

Emma began her speech along the same vein as those before her and Bonnie suddenly understood what was bothering her so much. This school needed something more than high achievers boasting of their works and presenting themselves as a step above others. They needed someone to be captain because they cared about them. As Emma concluded her speech it held a moment of hope for Bonnie.

'I promise to give everything I can to meet your needs.'

However, Bonnie's sigh of relief that someone actually wanted to give was short lived. Emma's final words took it away. 'I have worked hard to achieve many things for you, but being school captain would be an achievement which I would value more highly than all my others. I would be proud and honoured if you would vote for me.'

Taking a deep breath, Bonnie took the microphone while

each of the potential captains sat down and the applause rang through the auditorium. She waited for the applause to die down.

'Well, I don't know about you, but I felt just a bit intimidated when I heard those speeches.' She heard a few students chuckle at her frank comment. 'Us poor old normal people now need to get our average brains together and hope we're smart enough to make the right choice.'

More laughter came, while Mr Rush searched for his notes. He felt in all his pockets then glanced at Bonnie.

'Keep going there for a moment, Bonnie, I think I left my notes in my office. Entertain them a bit longer, will you?'

Bonnie looked out into the expectant faces before her and for the first time, she was sorry she had refused nomination. She spoke her thoughts out loud.

'I know that some of you nominated me, and I'm sorry I let you down by not thinking about what a real school captain is until I heard these speeches. You know, I would be neither proud nor honoured to be your school captain. That's why I refused the job.'

Glancing around at the curious eyes, she continued on. 'I know it's too late, but I would take the job very seriously and probably not even mention it on my resume, because I don't think it's about being a high achiever. I think it's about being approachable and travelling the same journey as the rest of you. That's why you nominated me, isn't it? Because I'm average like the rest of you. Well, I just want to take this opportunity to say I'm sorry I didn't realise you really wanted someone you could relate to, who would cope with the boring meetings thinking of you and not her resume, who would do her best to be a listening ear.'

She took another deep breath, seeing that she had stunned everyone. 'Choose wisely, students,' she said quietly. 'Choose the person you think will most understand you, represent you and care for *you*.'

With that she handed the microphone back to Mr Rush who had now returned. Before Mr Rush could speak, a student from the middle of the auditorium stood and began to clap. Bonnie noticed with embarrassment that it was Reece. But he was soon followed by many more students until the entire auditorium had burst into applause, including the teachers.

Mr Rush bent and spoke into her ear. 'Well, it's a pity you didn't decide earlier.'

She smiled in agreement. 'Perhaps.' Her smiled faded as she glanced at Emma's stricken face and realised what she had just done. 'I just hope I haven't created enemies amongst those who are running.'

He chuckled. 'Frankly, I don't care if you did. I'm hoping you have changed the whole face of school captain nominees for future years.'

The assembly broke up and the group made their way to class. She had to find Emma. There she was, rushing through the crowd of students, dodging whoever she could. Quickly, Bonnie raced after her and put a hand on her arm. Emma spun around and her eyes flashed sparks.

'What did you think you were doing, making fools of us like that?' She shook off Bonnie's hand. 'You weren't even running for captain so it was totally unnecessary.'

Bonnie was genuinely sorry. 'It wasn't about getting votes.'

'Obviously. But what was it about? Will you tell me that?' Emma's voice hissed and she was near to tears. 'Was it about getting Reece's attention?'

'Emma, that's not fair. Reece had nothing to do with it. I just spoke on the spur of the moment. I wasn't really thinking.'

Emma stopped walking and flung her arms across her chest. 'Well I'm sick of your little popularity game! Even if I get voted in I won't enjoy it now. I will know they really wanted you.'

'Emma, they will respect you if you live up to what they really need in a school captain.'

Emma was crying, now. 'I can't, Bonnie. I can't live up to everything you said today. All that psychological stuff about being one of them and being a listening ear. I've never been one of them. I'm a Christian for goodness' sake!'

Bonnie stared at her in stunned silence. Being a Christian didn't mean you couldn't listen to people, understand them and be down to earth!

'Emma, you are a listening ear!' Bonnie put out a hand but Emma moved out of reach. 'Remember when I first met you I couldn't help liking you! I've told you things about my past that I would never tell anyone else!'

Emma's countenance was beginning to soften at Bonnie's encouragement, when suddenly her face fell again and she bolted away. Turning, Bonnie saw the reason as Reece came to her side.

'Bonnie, that was great. Thank you.'

She shook her head dazedly. 'I don't think it was great at all. I just hurt Emma again and all because I didn't think enough before I spoke.'

Reece shook his head. 'No, Bonnie. I hurt Emma, not you.' Bonnie couldn't help her surprise showing as Reece continued, a faint blush filling his cheeks. 'She knows I have feelings for you.'

Bonnie swallowed hard. 'For me? Why?'

He seemed neither threatened nor surprised by her question. 'Lots of reasons. But I don't want to list them all here in the middle of the school corridor.'

Bonnie stared.

'Come on,' Reece laughed. 'I've just confessed my feelings for you and you're staring at me like I can't be serious.'

'That was what I was thinking,' she confessed as a student pushed past her. She was finding it hard to think, standing there with Reece gazing at her so intently and students rushing noisily past on their way to class. 'Do you know how old I am? About the fire?'

His eyes became tender as he smiled. 'I've heard, but true beauty goes deeper than the skin and true love defies time.'

She grinned. 'Wow, you're a poet!'

'Bonnie …' His tone was pleading now, and Bonnie forced herself to be serious. She didn't want to hurt yet another friend today. Praying desperately for the right words she took a deep breath and met his eyes.

'I admire your nice nature and your depth, Reece.' She hesitated. 'But … well, I can't love you like that right now.'

He smiled kind of sadly, 'I thought so.' He turned to go, then stopped and looked earnestly at her. 'Don't feel you have to avoid me or anything, Bonnie. The last thing I'd want is to have this affect your new relationship with God.'

'I won't let it,' Bonnie promised, impressed with him more than she ever had been before. She knew she was doing the right thing despite having some regrets, the main one being that she couldn't love him the way he wanted her to. But somewhere deep inside she knew she couldn't feel for him as she had once felt for Blaze. Perhaps she would never feel that way for anyone else again in her life.

* * *

Votes had been cast and counted. It had been hard to know how to vote but Bonnie finally decided on Emma. After all, Emma was a believer and had God's Holy Spirit to counsel her. Now Mr Rush had called her to his office and she stood looking around the room. Spread across his desk were voting forms the staff had obviously been counting. Mr Rush slid a piece of paper in front of Bonnie.

'Bonnie, I want you to take a look at this.'

Bonnie sat and picked it up. It was a voting form. On it were the five names of the nominees and beneath it, the voter had pencilled in another name and created a box beside it which was ticked. 'Bony Blaik' she read and laughed.

'That doesn't count because it's spelled wrong.' She gave a grin and shrugged. 'One of those poor, average students like me, I guess.'

Mr Rush, however, was not grinning. 'Bonnie, ninety percent of votes were cast this way.'

He pushed many more forms before her eyes with the same pencilled in name and ticked box.

'At least most of them spelled my name right,' she said absently, amazed by what she saw.

'Bonnie, no other person has ever received such a high percentage of votes. The staff have all discussed what to do, and we're going to break tradition. You didn't accept nomination before the closing date, but will you accept nomination now?'

'Can you break the rules like that?' Bonnie's blue eyes were wide.

'This is not a normal situation and yes, we can. Ninety percent of the student population will agree to the change of constitution for election of school captain this year. I think that allows us to bend the rules just this once, don't you?'

Bonnie nodded, feeling bewildered. 'I guess so, but what about the other nominees?'

'I've spoken to them and they have agreed to this.'

'Really?' Bonnie found it hard to believe after Emma's reaction.

He nodded. 'Yes, they can see that this isn't a slight on them, but rather a change in the way we view the role of school captain.'

Bonnie smiled. 'Well then, yes, I accept nomination.'

Mr Rush stood and held out his hand. 'You have my

congratulations, Captain. You may not feel proud and honoured to be school captain, but I will be proud to be principal while you are captain of this school.'

Chapter Twenty Eight

Bonnie began attending the youth Bible studies and found her faith growing as fast as her knowledge. Tonight as Aaron spoke, she sat poring over her Bible. The verse they were looking at didn't make much sense to her spiritually young mind. If only she could get her head around it. Her eyes wandered back to the start of the chapter. Quickly she read, and it was though her eyes were opened. Why hadn't Aaron asked them to read it in context? It would have made all the difference. She looked up to see Reece watching her. He copied her frown then smiled. Smiling back, she relaxed. Now that they had established a friendship she found his attention a lot less threatening.

'What do you think it means?' Aaron asked the group.

Bonnie read it again, then glanced around the group. No one seemed to have any answer.

'*My grace is sufficient for you. My power is made perfect in weakness.*' That verse on its own said very little.

'Maybe it's saying that God doesn't want to give us everything because then we would be like God,' Callie suggested. 'Us being weak makes God look even better.'

Bonnie found herself frowning again. That wasn't what she had understood it to mean at all. She didn't think God was like that. Aaron ignored Callie's answered and looked to Carl.

'What do you think, Carl?'

Carl looked up quickly and blushed. 'Sorry, where are we?'

'Two Corinthians twelve verse nine.'

Carl began to study the verse intently, embarrassed that he'd been caught watching Emma. To everyone's relief he was saved from the awkward moment when Sheree jumped in.

'I think it's saying to be satisfied with what we've got.'

Aaron nodded and smiled. 'I agree.'

Bonnie listened, her heart bothered. She wasn't sure whether to speak up or not. They had missed the whole point! Or had she missed the whole point? She needed to know.

'I'm not sure …' she ventured, trying to control her nerves.

'Which part aren't you sure about?' Aaron's voice was patronising as though he found it a bit irritating to have to explain deep concepts to a new believer.

'All of it. Sheree's right, but I think maybe there's a lot more to it. If we read the whole chapter—'

'We don't have time.' Aaron was clearly annoyed now, but Bonnie didn't give in.

'I'll summarise it. Paul seems to be saying he has plenty of things to boast about. He's talented and has good social standing. But then he says God gave him some kind of suffering and wouldn't take it away.' She took a deep breath and swallowed.

'I think this verse is saying that God is free to work in us once we recognise our weakness.' She stopped short as she saw Emma's look. She glanced to Aaron who had become slightly red in the face. He was either flustered or angry. She had obviously said too much.

'Go on,' Reece encouraged and Bonnie saw that all other eyes were watching her.

'Well, if we don't see our need, there is no room for God

in our lives. We use our own strengths and believe we deserve credit for everything we do.'

'But if we know we have a need we allow God to be our strength. We rely on Him for everything we do. And God can use our weaknesses more than *we* can ever use our own abilities.'

No one spoke until Aaron shifted. 'Can you put that simply?' he asked, his voice clipped.

'Basically, in this verse God is telling Paul that he allowed him to suffer because it made him look to God. And when we look to God for strength we can achieve more than we ever have before in our lives.'

Many eyes were lighting up as one by one they began to understand. Reece smiled wide, his eyes alight with understanding. 'I've never seen it so clearly before.'

Others nodded. 'Me either.'

'Yeah, it makes sense now.'

Bonnie smiled, glad she had made the effort despite Aaron's disapproval. She loved the way the Bible so often came to life and brought a depth and meaning to life she could never have imagined.

Bonnie was about to leave after the study when Aaron called her aside. 'Bonnie, I know this is all new and exciting for you, but you need to be careful to let me be the leader.'

Bonnie's eyes widened. 'You thought I was trying to take over?'

Still clearly ruffled, Aaron's voice rose in volume. 'You can't just come out in the middle of a study and accuse me of not looking at things in context. And you have to be so careful with God's Word, not to twist it. You put a whole different slant on that verse about God's grace being sufficient.'

Her heart sank. 'I was wrong?'

'Well, no, not exactly, but—' Aaron was cut off as his

father came out of the study. The door was just behind where Bonnie and Aaron stood. His face was a mixture of concern and understanding as he put a hand on his son's shoulder.

'Can you two come in here for a moment?'

Aaron looked unhappy as he moved stiffly into the office. Meekly, Bonnie followed. She had never felt more embarrassed in her life. If only she had kept her mouth shut, kept her ideas to herself.

Mr Mathison studied them both for a minute, then turned to Aaron. 'You felt Bonnie took over?'

He nodded, looking down at his shoes.

'Bonnie, did you interrupt someone?' She blushed and shook her head, no.

'Did you tell someone else they were wrong?'

'Well, no. I suggested they weren't looking at the full picture.'

Mr Mathison looked down at the copy of Aaron's notes he had on his desk. 'I thought the same thing, actually.'

Aaron jarred as though he had been slapped and his father put his hand on his shoulder again.

'I'm not saying you haven't done a good job. I just think we have some members of the group with gifts of insight and leadership that should be honed.'

With renewed confidence, Aaron nodded vigorously. 'Oh, I agree, but Bonnie seems to think she understands everything now she's a believer. Emma agrees with me. She doesn't seem to realise it takes years to grow and that you can't understand everything overnight.'

Deeply hurt, Bonnie fought the tears that sprang to her eyes. She was relieved when Mr Mathison dismissed Aaron, saying he would talk to him later. Then he faced Bonnie and his eyes were gentle. 'Have a seat.'

Bonnie sat.

'I'm sorry about that, Bonnie. I know I need to handle this very sensitively, but I want you to know how encouraged I am by your enthusiasm to learn more about God. I am also amazed by your understanding. You have a gift that way. Young Reece does, too. I know I wasn't there tonight, but I honestly don't believe you did anything wrong. Aaron has his own issues we need to work through … and Emma is having a bit of a rough time of it, too.' He shuffled a little uncomfortably, then met her eyes again. 'Can you do something for me?'

Bonnie simply nodded.

'I have been praying for a few weeks now for a youth pastor for our church. I'd like you to pray, too. We need someone who can concentrate full time on discipling and leading the young people in our church. Please pray with me for a young man who is humble; someone who can delight in the spiritual growth of others, who doesn't feel it threatens his own position. Will you pray that with me?'

Bonnie's eyes widened. 'Now?'

'If that's okay.'

Bonnie nodded and took a deep breath. What if she prayed the wrong thing? God would understand, but would Mr Mathison? Despite her fear, she began. 'Lord, you know what we need. You know who we need. Please provide the right person …' She struggled to remember Mr Mathison's requirements. 'Someone humble who can help us grow to know and love you more. Just … well, the right one, please.'

'Amen,' Mr Mathison agreed. 'Lord, I believe you already have someone set apart for us, so please lead me to him! And Lord, thank you for Bonnie and the gifts you have given her. Help her to continue to grow and take joy in you. Amen.'

Bonnie opened her eyes and smiled, her joy restored. Mr Mathison smiled back. It was all going to be okay now. She no longer felt hurt by Aaron and Emma's treatment of her. Rather, she felt the need to pray for them; to love them and continue to be their friend. Mr Mathison's suggestion to pray about the situation had been the best solution for all. Now she could leave it all in God's capable hands.

Chapter Twenty Nine

Bonnie could see that Emma was having a hard time and she continued to pray. Still, the way Emma avoided her cut deep. She sat down on the back step of her home and buried her head in her hands. She often came here to pray and try to sort out her mind.

'What do I do, Lord?'

This time the answer came. 'Go to her.'

It wasn't an audible voice but it was clear. Bonnie knew she had heard God speak to her and gave a little chuckle.

'Okay, Lord, now I'm really weird like Blaze. I always thought it was really out there to believe you would speak. But you have ...'

Even thinking about approaching Emma had her heart racing, but she knew she had to do it. Now.

'Lord, give me the words to speak. Don't let me hurt her more.'

Emma's expression was wary when she invited Bonnie inside. Bonnie took her usual seat, finding it hard to look directly into Emma's eyes when they held so much pain. She took a deep breath.

'Emma, I'm sorry I hurt you.'

Emma raised an eyebrow. 'You hurt me? What are you talking about?'

'My thoughtless words. My actions … everything that's caused you so much pain. Is there anything I can do to fix it up? I miss you and the friendship we had.'

Emma's expression softened as she licked dry lips. 'You didn't hurt me.' Her voice came out hoarse. 'I hurt myself.'

'What do you mean?'

Emma shrugged and her face began to crumple. 'Having all these dreams about Reece when they were hopeless …'

'Is that really what this is all about? Reece?'

Emma's shoulders shook. 'In a way. When Reece started taking an interest in you I suddenly saw you as the competition. I guess I started looking for bad things about you to make myself feel better.' She gave a half sob, half laugh. 'It didn't work. I felt even worse. But it's okay now, I confessed it to God and He's forgiven me. I, well, I just didn't know how to talk to you about it.'

Bonnie took a deep breath. 'Emma, you don't need to compete with me. Reece and I are not involved.'

'You're not? I thought … well, you two are so close … I just presumed.'

'We've never been more than friends. He's too young for me. Not in maturity, but in other ways. He's nice, but he's not for me.'

Emma's eyes widened in surprise, then she broke down completely. 'Bonnie, I hate the way I've been. I hate the way I've treated you and I haven't been able to pray or enjoy reading the Bible. I wouldn't have believed one guy could so drastically affect my relationship with God and other people.'

'Everyone's human, Emma. Even you,' Bonnie let out a chuckle, 'though when I first met you, I wondered. Sometimes you seemed *too* perfect.'

Emma smiled then, through tears, took a shuddering breath then straightened her shoulders.

'Don't give up Reece just for me. I'll be okay. Really.'

'I'm not giving him up for you,' Bonnie assured. 'I have other reasons. Reece and I have talked about it and we're just friends. We're both okay with that.'

With that, Emma threw her arms around her. 'I've never had a friend quite like you! You're a gift from God!'

'I think the same about you!' Bonnie couldn't help beaming as a load rolled from her shoulders. She finally had her friend back.

* * *

Mr Mathison stood before the church congregation and smiled around. 'Our answer to prayer has arrived. God has led us to a young man who will take on the spiritual needs of our youth.'

Bonnie's heart leapt with hope. Already? Mr Mathison had found a man he could trust? She had been praying but hadn't expected an answer so soon.

'As soon as the church leadership met him we knew.' Mr Mathison informed the congregation. 'We prayed and the sense became stronger. We appointed him immediately.' Mr Mathison met Bonnie's eyes for a moment, then his eyes swept the congregation again as his smile grew.

'He's a trainee still completing his Bible college degree but we believe this is of benefit to us all. He is a remarkable young man with a great love and concern for the youth of this country, and he needs an opportunity to put his training into practice under the mentorship of another pastor. I am personally thrilled to be able to work with him.'

So this young man was special? He had clearly impressed Mr Mathison. Bonnie looked forward to meeting him and despite her guilt at the thought, hoped he was nothing like Aaron Mathison. It was hard to be learning about the God who loved her when the leader so clearly disliked her. She just wanted to be free to learn and express her joy at the exciting things God revealed.

'The youth will have an opportunity to meet him on

Wednesday in their school lunch break. He will be taking over the Bible question time we have begun in the past few weeks.'

Bonnie smiled. Well, that would certainly throw the trainee pastor in the deep end. But it would also give a good indication of his ability to lead and deal with youth. Some of her peers asked questions that would throw any experienced theologian. She looked forward to seeing what would happen and found her heart beating faster with anticipation as Wednesday lunch time approached. The closer it came the more she felt that something significant was about to happen. She deliberately slowed her actions as the lunch bell went.

'Bonnie, we haven't got much time left to get to the meeting,' Emma urged. Bonnie deliberately packed another item from her desk into her pencil case and gave Emma a cheeky grin.

'Anyone would think you were desperate to meet this young minister, Emma. Aren't you content with Reece anymore?'

Emma grinned back, putting her hands on her hips. 'I've already met the guy, Bon. And to be honest, I'm doing it for your sake – in case you haven't noticed, you're getting old and you're still single.'

Laughing and pretending to throw the pencil case at her, Bonnie allowed herself to hurry. They could hear voices as they raced down the school hall. Bonnie wondered where they came from. It couldn't possibly be from the meeting room. They were lucky to get two or three people to their school Bible question times. However, as they came closer it became clear the room was filled with students. Male and female voices could be heard chatting, trying to be heard above one another. Bonnie turned to Emma.

'Hey, there's heaps of people in there!'

The room quieted as they prepared to enter and a voice could be heard asking the youth pastor a question.

'Mr Clements, do you still ride horses?'

Bonnie stopped dead while Emma continued into the room without glancing behind her.

'Not as often,' Bonnie heard a deep voice reply, 'though I still enjoy riding.'

She would recognise that voice anywhere.

'You can call me Blaze – I'm not that much older than any of you.' The voice was so warm and familiar Bonnie wanted to laugh and cry all at once. She couldn't think, didn't know what to do.

'Isn't Bonnie Blake coming?' a student asked Emma and in a flash Bonnie disappeared back around the corner and into the spare classroom. What on earth was going on? Blaze Clements *here*?

* * *

Emma finally found Bonnie in the library where she had spent the lunch hour just sitting, staring at her hands. 'Where did you get to, Bonnie? Got the last minute jitters?'

Bonnie had no answer and looking closer at her pale face, Emma's eyes suddenly dawned understanding. 'Is it because of the horses?'

'What do you mean?' Bonnie tried to sound puzzled, but her hoarse, dry throat gave it away.

'You were rescuing a horse when you got burned and this guy was talking about the circus and his horses. Is it still hard to think about horses?'

Bonnie nodded, and Emma put a protective arm around her. 'They're going to give it to you, the students,' she warned. 'Mr Clements was really interested in where you disappeared to. They all kept telling him he'd really like you and he just got this funny smile on his face.'

Bonnie heard Laura and Reece coming down the hall and closed her eyes, hugging her arms across her chest. The moment they entered the library their faces broke into wide grins.

'You've sure got a way of making people like you, Bonnie. Even when they've never met you!' Laura lifted her hands in mock exasperation. 'That good looking circus man didn't want to know about anybody but our school captain, Bonnie Blake!'

Bonnie listened in stunned silence. It was true. Blaze was here – and he was the new youth pastor. How could she concentrate on class now? But she had no choice. She had to pull herself together and go.

'You all right?' Emma threw on her backpack.

Bonnie stopped in her tracks, still feeling dazed. Was she all right? Not really. She couldn't think, couldn't put her words together. 'I don't think I am okay. Emma, I need to talk with you.'

'Okay, let's go into the study.'

As they rounded the corner to the study, Bonnie stopped short again. He was somewhere close by. She could hear his voice. There was a pleasant cheerfulness to it, so why did she feel so heavy? Would she never escape the awful ugliness of what had happened? The shame, the change in her nature. Was she really ready to face Blaze Clements with a fiance or wife – Blaze and Shelley?

'Quick!' She grabbed Emma's arm and urged her past the door and into the study. Then she slammed the door shut and stood looking wild-eyed at Emma. Safe at last.

'Bonnie, what is going on?' Emma's eyes were wide with shock. 'You're acting like he's a murderer or something. Do you know him?'

She nodded, then shaking, motioned for Emma to sit down. 'Yes, Emma, I know him. There's so much I haven't told you ...'

Emma listened, wide-eyed as Bonnie began the story, starting with the day the unusual Clements family had turned up at school to the fire and the way it had changed her.

'Oh, Bonnie, I had no idea!'

Bonnie found her own eyes strangely dry despite the tears now running unchecked down Emma's cheeks.

'You need to talk with him, Bonnie.'

Slowly, sadly, she shook her head. 'I can't. I'm not ready. I don't know if I will ever be ready.'

'But you believe now! Everything's different.'

'I'm still burned and ugly.' Sadness enveloped her as she spoke the words. It was the truth as much as she hated to acknowledge it.

'You're not ugly, Bonnie! Especially not on the inside! And no one with blue eyes and a smile like yours can be called ugly, no matter how scarred they are.' Her expression turned sheepish. 'Why do you think I was so jealous of you?'

The study door opened and both pairs of eyes flew to Emma's father.

'Bonnie, there you are!'

'Mr Mathison.'

'Bonnie, an old friend of yours is here and would like to see you. You remember Blaze?'

Did she remember Blaze? Emma slipped discreetly out the door, while Bonnie made a grab at her hand. How could she answer a question like that? How could Emma have left her at a time like this?

Mr Mathison stepped aside and the tall figure behind him stepped in. Bonnie didn't miss the way Mr Mathison slipped away just as his daughter had done and her heart pounded in her chest. Sowly, she allowed her eyes to focus on Blaze Clements.

He was taller. And older. The boy with all his pimples had gone and a young man stood in his place. She smiled slightly, remembering the way she had assured the insecure teenager that his pimples would disappear. She had been right. From the top of his dark head and tidy clothes, down to his feet in shoes, not riding boots, Blaze Clements as a man was definitely not unattractive.

'Bonnie!' His deep voice was joyful and her eyes flew to his. Still dark and incredibly intense, they captured her. He had an undeniable presence that seemed to dominate everything else in the room.

'How are you, Blaze?' She could think of nothing better to say. All sensible thoughts had flown from her mind.

He grinned and it lit up his manly face, drawing attention to his strong jawline. 'It's not like you to resort to small talk.'

She chuckled and tried to ignore the tremor in her laugh. What was the right thing to say? She had no idea. There were so many things she could say but they were all racing through her mind so fast she couldn't pick out which one to speak.

He took a step forward. 'It's been a while, Miss Perfect.'

His voice was deeper than she remembered. There was teasing in his tone and she knew he was trying to make her relax. It didn't work. She still couldn't work out what to say. It seemed that he couldn't, either. They just stared at one another until he hesitantly took another step then lowered himself down beside her. He shuffled, absently playing with his shirt sleeves and she saw the way his eyes moved to her hands. Scarred hands. He swallowed a few times and began to say something then stopped, clearing his throat. She noted with relief there was no wedding ring on his finger. He hadn't married Shelley yet. Disconcerted, she sat on her hands to stop them shaking as much as to hide them. He was really here.

'I had no idea it would be you,' she finally managed. 'They said they were getting a trainee youth pastor, but ...' she shrugged, 'well, I just didn't think. Not even when Emma said the new youth pastor was young and ...' She blushed.

'Young and what?'

She couldn't look at him. 'Umm, good looking. She said you were good looking, not that I'm saying that I should have … never mind.'

He was looking at her with amused interest, now. 'I'm sorry. I probably should have warned you.'

Her eyes flew to his in surprise. 'That you were good looking?'

He let out such a laugh that she couldn't help joining in. 'No,' he was still chuckling. 'I should have warned you I was coming.'

'You knew I was here?'

'Mr Mathison couldn't stop talking about you. You seem to make quite an impact wherever you go.'

She didn't respond and Blaze's eyes burned into hers. 'I wish you'd tell me what you are thinking, Bonnie. What's going on in that amazing mind of yours?'

She swallowed hard. 'Do you think we could talk sometime soon? Without Shelley?'

He frowned. 'Without Shelley?'

This was going to be harder than she thought, but it would be almost impossible to sort things out with Shelley there.

'I came to see you in hospital, Blaze.'

He looked pained. 'And I didn't recognise you?'

'You didn't see me. I left before anyone knew I was there.'

Blaze frowned, clearly puzzled. His hand reached to take hers, his touch sending shock waves through her. She pulled her hand out from beneath his. 'I saw you and Shelley there, Blaze. Together. And I heard the doctor say you were going to make it. I just couldn't … well, I don't know …' She stumbled on her words, realising she couldn't explain what drove her away.

Understanding filled his eyes. 'Bonnie, Shelley and I are not together.'

Her eyes darted to his, revealing more than she wanted them to.

'We're good friends and we studied together in Bible college, but she was always in love with Tom, her childhood friend. They're married.'

Bonnie frowned. 'I saw Sky …'

'Prince's little one? Tom and Shelley are fostering her. Carrie abandoned her and Prince didn't want her. I'm her legal guardian but I don't want her growing up without a mother figure like I did, so I asked Tom and Shelley to foster her for the time being.' His eyes sparkled and he let out a deep chuckle. 'Shelley was just bringing her in to visit me at the hospital.'

Bonnie wondered what he found funny about her mistake. Or was it the thought of being married that put the twinkle in his eyes? It was a reasonable mistake to make, wasn't it? He was very young, but the Clements family had never done things the 'normal' way.

A bell sounded somewhere in the school, reminding them where they were. Blaze stood to his full height. 'You're right. We need to catch up …' His mouth widened into a grin. 'Without Shelley since she's got nothing to do with this.' He reached a hand to help her up and this time she didn't feel uncomfortable at his touch. 'How about tonight, or do you have a date with *your* fiance?'

Seeing the amusement in his eyes, she gave a good-natured grin. 'No.'

'Well, how about we go somewhere private where he's not likely to run into us. I'll find a nice restaurant.'

Bonnie laughed and agreed to let him pick her up and take her out for tea. She was about to leave when she suddenly turned back and looked deep into his eyes. 'Hey, Blaze.' Her voice became soft. 'Thanks for praying for me all those years ago.'

His face lit into a brilliant smile. 'My pleasure, Bonnie Blake. It was worth every prayer I prayed.'

* * *

Emma found Bonnie in the girls' change rooms just staring in the mirror with a bewildered expression.

'Are you okay? What happened?'

Bonnie turned from the mirror to face her friend. 'I'm going to catch up with him some more tonight … and he's not engaged after all.'

Emma grinned with delight. 'Oh, Bonnie, God is incredible the way he unfolds his plan in our lives! Who would have imagined this?'

'It's not like that, Emma.'

'I'm sure it is! You admitted that he used to love you but couldn't do anything about it because you weren't a Christian. Now you are!'

'I'm not the girl he loved, Emma. I've changed.' Bonnie turned back to the mirror. The differences were there. Not even subtle. 'He cares about me and will protect me – love me as a sister and that's it. For a start, I weigh ten kilograms more. I'm quieter and covered in scars. I'm not the same person. I can't expect anything to be the same.'

'If you weighed ten kilograms less you must have been a rake!' Emma exclaimed. 'You're not overweight!'

Despite Emma's reassurance, Bonnie was ashamed of the reflection she saw in the mirror. She could no longer see a slim, attractive teenager with a happy 'unrefined' nature staring back at her. She needed to take up athletics again. She couldn't lounge around and expect to still look the way she did when she was fifteen.

'Bonnie,' Emma put a hand on her friends shoulder, 'don't put yourself down. Be the new person God has made you. There is no reason Blaze wouldn't love you just the way you are.'

Bonnie said nothing. Emma hadn't known her years before.

How could she know the extent of difference between the girl who had freely laughed and teased Blaze and the reflection that now stared back with serious blue eyes?

God, please help me cope with this! Help me see Blaze as just a friend.

Chapter Thirty

Bonnie tried to calm her nerves as she heard a car pull up out the front and Blaze's footsteps come to the door. 'You never used to be nervous with him,' she berated herself, 'and you're still good friends, so get a hold of yourself!'

Her mother opened the door and gave the tall young man a hug, excitedly telling him how wonderful it was to see him. However, it was clear he was distracted. He gave Mrs Blake enough acknowledgement not to be rude, then allowed his eyes to sweep the room. His face lit into a smile when he found Bonnie.

'You ready?'

She nodded, hoping she wasn't too dressed up, nor underdressed. With relief she noted that Blaze's mode of dress was smart but casual. In fact, he looked tidier than she remembered seeing him before.

'Someone taught him some dress sense,' she thought with a wry smile. He walked down the path slightly ahead of her, inclining his head so their eyes could meet.

'I rang Johnny and Misty to tell them I've found you.' He sounded almost apologetic and Bonnie's mouth turned up as he opened the car door for her then closed it again. He walked around to the driver's side and lowered himself into the car. 'I just couldn't wait to tell them. Misty was so delighted when I told her you've become a Christian. She burst into tears on the phone.'

'Misty is a believer?' Bonnie searched for the seat belt clip.

'Yeah, she is now.' Blaze reached over and took the seat belt from her hand, clicking it into place. 'Sorry, it's an awkward belt. I bought this car cheap because it's falling apart.' He did up his own seat belt and started the ignition. It was a strange feeling to be sitting beside him like this in a car. Blaze belonged with horses, not machines. He always had.

'Misty's doing really well. She's got a job training horses. She's always been clumsy in everyday life, but she's so nimble and talented when it comes to horses.'

Bonnie smiled, enjoying Blaze's full speed talking. Was he nervous? She was. She focused on his muscular arms on the steering wheel. He really had grown from a boy into a man. She wondered if she had changed, too. Maybe her fuller figure was actually the natural change from a girl to a woman? She tried to pay attention to what he was saying.

'Storm is still an angry young man. He's working on the roads but isn't happy doing anything really. Prince is living with his girlfriend from uni. Starre's at uni, too. And Beauty is causing trouble at the moment. Dad's just about given up on her.'

Bonnie listened hungrily to all the news. She had tried to shut the Clements family out of her heart and mind for so long, but deep inside she had been longing for them; longing to know how they were going and yearning to see them. Blaze pulled into the restaurant car park and turned off the motor. He turned to her with a sheepish grin. 'It's gone quiet suddenly. Is that because the car's stopped or because I've stopped?'

Bonnie unfastened her seatbelt and threw him a cheeky

look. 'I wouldn't dare say.'

He waited for her to join him around his side of the car. 'Chicken.'

He locked the car then reached for her hand and led her into the restaurant. His hand felt warm and strong around hers and she wondered at how protected she felt. But could he feel her scars? Did they bother him?

He pulled a chair out for her at a table for two and then sat opposite, casting her a smile. 'I'm getting used to the middle-class Aussie lifestyle.' He passed her a menu. 'I felt so out of place the first time I went to a restaurant, but I'm not a circus boy anymore!'

'I see you've changed your clothing style, too.'

'Yeah. You taught me well.'

'I taught you?' Flustered, she fiddled with the serviette beside her cutlery and avoided looking at him.

'Don't you remember the shopping trip?' There was a smile in his voice. 'I might have pretended I wasn't listening, but I was. Your style grew on me.'

Bonnie tried to calm herself as she looked up. He smiled again in a disarming manner. 'Don't tell me you've forgotten our times together?'

Her heart beat wildly in her chest. 'No ... although I tried to for a while.'

His look became compassionate, all teasing gone. 'Why? Because of the fire?'

His eyes were too intense at that moment, but their magnetic nature kept her from turning away.

'It wasn't totally the fire,' she admitted. 'It was the way I said goodbye – how it all finished. With me causing you hurt because I didn't believe, and you being ... well, you seemed ... I don't know.' She opened and shut her mouth again. Opened it and shut it again. She saw his gentle smile.

'What are you wanting to say?'

She shrugged, and his hand reached out and covered hers. 'I'd like to know.'

She nodded, taking the plunge. She had to overcome her fear. 'I couldn't stand the way you lost respect for me when I rode Peter Pan; but I couldn't blame you, either.'

Blaze's dark eyes widened. 'What made you think I lost respect for you?'

'You were so angry. I hated leaving, knowing you were angry with me, but I couldn't stay, either.'

Blaze's expression was pained as he shook his head. 'I'm so sorry, my Bonnie.' His voice became deep and low. 'You've lived all this time thinking I was angry with you.'

Bonnie tried to understand his reaction. His eyes sparkled in the light and she wondered if it could possibly be the glisten of tears. The huskiness of his voice in the next moment gave her the answer.

'I was afraid for you and felt pain for you. I wasn't angry. I just wanted to take you into my arms and hold you tight until you could know you were loved, weakness, scars and all. I'm sorry I seemed angry and that it drove you away.'

Did he mean he had loved her scars and all? Immediately she dismissed the idea with regret. He was talking about God loving her.

'I missed your friendship,' she confessed, wishing she could meet his eyes, but afraid of him reading the depth of feeling in her own. 'Every other friendship just seemed so ... empty. Like something was missing. Meeting God took a lot of that emptiness away, though.'

'And meeting Reece?'

Bonnie's eyes darted to his. 'Who told you about Reece?'

'He did.'

Bonnie fell silent for a moment, then shook her head. 'Emma and Reece belong together.'

To her surprise, Blaze laughed a gentle, amused laugh. 'That's crazy. If you love someone, you don't let them go just because your friend has feelings for them.'

'Exactly!' Her look was triumphant. 'That proves I'm not in love with him!'

Blaze's eyes were amused as he shook his head and ruffled her hair across the table. It reminded her of the way she used to ruffle Storm's hair. It was an affectionate gesture, but it seemed very big brotherly and confident.

'How's the fish?' Blaze asked as Bonnie fumbled with her cutlery. She tried to swallow the remnants of what was in her mouth before answering.

'Not too bad.' She had no idea how she was going to get through the rest of the meal with him sitting directly across from her.

'The veal was good.' He indicated his empty plate. She laughed quietly, then watched in surprise as he reached across and took a piece of lettuce from her plate.

'Is this bad manners?'

She nodded. 'Yes, but I don't mind.' In fact, she was relieved. She had begun to think they would be there all night and she would still only be half way through her meal. She picked through the food on her plate until Blaze had managed to leave it empty.

'You still have perfect manners, don't you?' He grinned at her cutlery neatly placed together on her plate.

'It wouldn't hurt you to learn some, too.'

'I have.' He put on a hurt look but his eyes gave him away. 'They wouldn't let me finish my first year of Bible college without proving I could visit people without totally shocking them with my manners.'

Bonnie smiled, remembering his family's eating habits around the campfire all those years ago. 'I think your manners have improved,' she relented. 'They're definitely more refined.'

'Thank you.' He chuckled and went to pay the bill. He didn't even bother suggesting dessert after the way she picked through her first course and she was relieved. Nerves had a tight hold on her stomach and there was little room left in there for food.

'Thank you for an enjoyable evening,' she said politely as he walked her to her front door. He stopped with a laugh and put his arm around her shoulder. 'Hey, no need to be so formal! I'll start thinking I've seriously offended you if you speak like that.'

She laughed with him as she tried to think clearly enough to come up with a suitable response. Before she could, he turned and gave her a fierce hug.

'I'm so glad God caused our paths to cross again, Bonnie. I missed your friendship and I'm hoping we can now be even better friends than we were before.'

'Me too,' she whispered as her heart soared. Did he have any idea of the longings in her heart as she felt his strong arms around her? Could he possibly feel the same way?

He stepped back and smiled into her eyes. 'As Christians we have an eternal friendship. Nothing can take it away.'

Her heart fell. That's what he meant. Their friendship was deeper because they were both believers, now. Nothing more.

Chapter Thirty One

'Can I walk home with you?'

Bonnie started at the voice behind her at the school gate. It was Blaze.

'For old times' sake.' He gave an appealing smile.

She nodded and handed him her school bag with a roguish look. 'Walking with me has a price, so here you go.' His presence was a lot easier to cope with in the daylight. He took her bag without a word and fell into step beside her.

She smiled up at him. 'Emma tells me you're leading our Bible study groups now. So will you be there tonight?'

'Yeah, I'll be there. I won't be leading tonight, though. I'll just be getting the feel of it. It's all part of my practical training for the Bible college course. I'll watch Aaron tonight, and then Mr Mathison will assess me as I lead the one after that. Then I'll be on my own.'

Her eyes sparkled as she gave him a teasing look. 'So how do you deal with disruptive students?'

He didn't miss a beat. 'I threaten to kiss them.'

She hadn't expected that and felt heat rising up her face. The more she tried to stop it the hotter she felt. Blaze turned to look at her and gave a hearty laugh. 'How the tables have turned! Now is my time for revenge, Bonnie Blake!'

She wished she could hide the embarrassment he was so clearly enjoying. 'What do you mean?'

'Don't you remember how you showed me no pity in your teasing when we first met? Don't you remember the poor maiden who wanted a knight to rescue her but refused to let him kiss her until he had a horse?'

Bonnie blushed even deeper, but couldn't help laughing. 'You're being mean. I wouldn't have been so cruel.'

'You were! You knew I cared and you played on it.'

He seemed more amused than anything and Bonnie wondered how he could speak about it so comfortably. He obviously didn't feel the same way now.

'I always wanted you to believe in Jesus Christ because I loved you so much,' he said and she nodded, knowing that he had loved her. The way she loved Laura and Jayne and all her friends – with depth and a longing to see them walking with God.

'I don't think you understand what I'm saying.' Blaze was now serious. She heard the urgency in his tone. His eyes captured hers and threatened to overwhelm her. 'It wasn't just brotherly love, Bonnie. I was so attracted to you it drove me crazy!'

There it was. He had loved her once. Her throat tightened. 'I'm sorry for the pain I put you through.'

He smiled then. 'The pain is over. I've found you again and you know God. Finally, Bonnie, you believe!'

He gave her an impulsive hug that was almost too much for her to bear. She wondered if he had any idea how much his touch affected her. He seemed to have no idea and she would do everything within her power to make sure it stayed that way.

* * *

Bonnie deliberately avoided sitting next to Blaze in the youth

Bible study and concentrated on her usual battle with Aaron and Emma for the black bean bag. She gave Blaze a quick smile, but refused to allow herself the pleasure of gazing at him and soaking up his presence there that night. She had never felt so nervous about a Bible study. The night at the restaurant had created this same feeling. It must have been the night time that affected her. Maybe she was just tired and everything would be back to normal in the morning.

Mr Mathison introduced Blaze to the group and then handed the study over to Aaron for the last time. The passage studied was at the end of John, and soon Bonnie was fully involved. She loved the book of John and had read it several times in the past month, soaking up every detail.

Aaron handed around a sheet of questions and began. 'What do you think was happening when Jesus died?'

'He was paying for our sins.' Danielle gave her usual up-front answer.

'And he was rejected by God because He now bore our sin.' Reece squinted as he skimmed the page for the exact verse. Without thinking, Bonnie glanced up to see Blaze gazing at her. Feeling herself become warm under that gaze she quickly bent back down to look at the passage again, a furrow of concentration in her brow. Aaron looked over at that moment and saw her frown.

'What do you think, Bonnie?'

Relieved he seemed to be giving her a fair go, Bonnie tried to concentrate. 'It seems to be talking about the breaking of God Himself.' Her mind began to work and her voice showed her awe. 'Jesus and the Father and Holy Spirit were complete as God, but when Jesus took our sin, he couldn't be God anymore and ruined the whole relationship. He couldn't be God because he wasn't perfect anymore and God can't be anything but perfect.'

'I don't think Jesus was ever not God,' Aaron cut in a little icily. Bonnie fell silent, but as usual, Reece encouraged her to go on – this time with the support of Emma.

'I wasn't saying he wasn't God.' Bonnie licked dry lips as she became aware of the scrutiny of the group. 'I was saying he was no longer accepted as part of the Godhead because he had the sin of the whole world on his shoulders. Not only was his body destroyed – his whole identity was, too.'

She shook her head. 'I can't even imagine what He went through. I mean, when my body was burned, I still at least had my identity. The fire couldn't touch who I am deep inside. It couldn't change that I was the much loved daughter of the Blakes. But Jesus gave up everything! Even his identity!'

Bonnie glanced around then and Blaze's eyes caught hers. His expression was one of wonder and she knew it must be strange listening to her speak about God when she had once firmly believed she had no need of Him.

'I don't know that God meant us to glean all that information from those few words, "My God why have you forsaken me?"' Aaron sat up taller to regain control. 'What Jesus has done is way beyond our understanding and if we think we know it all, we have a lot to learn.'

Bonnie knew his remark was pointed at her but was glad he hadn't totally disregarded her answer as he sometimes did. She glanced toward Blaze and was astounded to see the anger on his face. He was glaring directly at Aaron. What was that about? Had he picked up Aaron's barb?

She was drawn back as Aaron spoke to her. 'Bonnie, would you read the next passage out, since you enjoy talking?' His voice wasn't altogether friendly. Bonnie chose to ignore it, but it seemed to be the final straw for Blaze.

'I hardly think Bonnie's been disruptive, Aaron,' he said and there was ice in his tone.

'I wasn't suggesting that.' Aaron gave Blaze a cold glare. The two exchanged a long look before Aaron turned back to Bonnie. 'Do you mind reading?'

'No.' Her voice came out small, but as she began to read her confidence grew. At least this was Aaron's last study and she wouldn't have to face him anymore. He thanked her politely for reading, then continued with the questions. Bonnie couldn't concentrate. Blaze's presence was too disconcerting.

She couldn't study in this group anymore. Not with Blaze being so brotherly and protective and her own heart responding with far more depth than he was encouraging. How on earth was she going to explain that to Blaze? She needed to get out the door as soon as the study finished. Away from Blaze. Away from Aaron. The door was open and she had a few seconds to make her escape. She wasn't fast enough. Blaze seemed to have known what she was going to do and caught her arm.

'Bonnie, can I come back to your place? I need to talk to you.'

She couldn't help the sigh that escaped. 'I'm sorry, Blaze, but I'm feeling really tired. Can I meet you tomorrow?'

His eyes searched hers and she saw his disappointment before he stepped back. 'Sure. Well, I'll see you then.'

'At my place? After school?'

He nodded and she was aware that he watched her as she left, but she was too tired to think sensibly tonight. What she had to tell him could be put off until tomorrow in the brightness of calm daylight. The storm of her emotions were blowing into a gale and she needed time to think.

Chapter Thirty Two

Bonnie listened to the knock on the door, knowing her mother would answer and then retreat into the garden to leave her with Blaze. Her mother was good at knowing when to make herself inconspicuous. She would go outside and pray just as Bonnie had asked her to.

'Lord, help me with this, please.' Bonnie took a deep breath and opened the door.

Blaze seemed to know something serious was going on and met her gaze evenly as she led him inside. He sat down, his eyes never leaving hers. 'You look like you've had a bad day.'

She sat across from him, wringing her hands, eyes down. 'In a way.' She started when he shifted to sit beside her. Her heart beat faster at his closeness. His arm was resting against hers and he turned to look directly at her.

'Bonnie, I'm so sorry for last night.' He waited for her eyes to meet his. 'I just hated the way that guy treated you, but I had no right to embarrass you like that and make it obvious to the whole group that I care about you.'

Care was such a mild word. She cared about her acquaintances. She even cared about her car.

'I've upset you, haven't I?' His expression was pained and

she knew she needed to be honest. Deep breaths should help. When she had pulled herself together enough she spoke.

'I'm struggling a bit, but it's not your fault. I'm thinking I should probably find another church, another youth group.'

'You're going to leave?' Blaze leapt to his feet, his look incredulous. 'Just when I've finally found you again?' Slowly, keeping his eyes on her face she saw him work at calming himself as he sat down. He rubbed his forehead in an agitated way. 'Why? Why would you leave now, Bonnie? Because of me?'

She was lost for words as her eyes begged him to understand. He took her hand and she knew he could feel her trembling.

'You're so different,' he whispered, and her throat tightened. That was why he could never love her. He used to love the old Bonnie, and now – now everything was so different – she was so different. She worked to fight the tears as she stared at her scarred hand.

'Bonnie, what is it? What have I done? Please tell me.'

If she could just get the words past the tightness in her throat she would be able to make him understand. But the more she tried, the more she felt tears gathering behind her eyes. She didn't want to break down. Not now.

'Bonnie?' His eyes were gentle despite their intensity. She had to explain.

'Everything has changed, Blaze.' The tears betrayed her and ran down her face. 'Once it was me who was confident – who had no time to notice you loved me, no concerns over appearance … and now look at me. Burned and unattractive. And you're so – so strong, so good looking, so confident and I'm falling apart because I'm in love with you.'

There. She'd said it.

Blaze said nothing for a time. He appeared deep in thought as his eyes searched her tear filled ones. Slowly he sat back and stretched his legs in front of him. He looked relaxed – as though a great load had just rolled off his shoulders.

'So, you're saying you think you should leave because you love me – and you don't think I can love you now that you have changed so much? You think that your burns are so distracting that it's too hard for me to look past them and be attracted to who you really are – the part of you that lasts forever?'

She nodded, seeing that he finally understood, but wondering at the smile that was playing about his mouth.

'I haven't made myself clear, have I?' He reached for her hand, then tucked a stray strand of hair behind her ear.

Confusion washed over her. She had to move back – get away from him. She couldn't think with him so close. She stood, but he stood, too. She went to step back, but he grasped her upper arms fiercely and held her before him. His eyes searched hers desperately.

'I love you so much, Bonnie. Every moment I'm thinking of you – wanting to be with you. I know your burns aren't attractive, but I can see past them! God has healed me as much as he healed you. I was angry and found it hard to cope when I first saw you after the accident. I believe God gave us time apart so we could adjust to the trauma we've been through.'

She gasped and saw he had even surprised himself. As she searched his face, his passionate expression softened. 'I mean that,' he confirmed slowly and with confidence, 'with all my heart.'

With relief as much as anything, she cried harder, trying to apologise for her tears. Smiling, he reached out and wiped them away. Her hand came up to touch his which was now resting gently on her cheek.

'I don't mind your tears, Bonnie.' He held her hand with both of his. 'Your tears, your hurts, your hesitancy – it's all beautiful to me, now that you are healing. They are what brought you to know

God! If I had a choice – the unscarred Bonnie who didn't know God, or this new Bonnie who is burned but who knows God, I would definitely choose the Bonnie who knows God.'

In that moment, more healing took place in Bonnie's heart and mind. She stared up at Blaze out of wide blue eyes, unable to believe what she was hearing.

A sheepish expression passed over his face. 'I don't know how a man asks a woman to be … his … well, his girlfriend.'

She shrugged, teasing coming into her moist eyes. 'Well, we all know you've never been good at knowing socially acceptable behaviour.'

A tender smile lighted his face. 'Will you allow me to get to know you more?' He ran his finger along the scars on her hand and waited for her answer.

'Can you really cope with my appearance?' She had to make sure.

'Cope?' He chuckled. 'I can more than cope! There's a lot more to you than your scars. Please just answer my question.'

She smiled wide into his eyes. She simply couldn't help it. 'I can't think of anything I want more. Yes, Blaze, yes.' Her heart beat faster as his head lowered, his dark eyes watching her every expression like a hawk. He stopped just millimetres from her mouth.

'Can I kiss you, my Bonnie?'

Feeling his warm breath on her skin, she nodded and closed her eyes. His lips touched hers gently at first, before his kiss deepened. She had never experienced anything like it. Sighing with contentment, she put her arms around him and held him tight. When she opened her eyes he was looking at her with that familiar intensity she so loved in him. Overwhelmed, she let out another sigh and smiled. 'I love you …. and I even loved you all those years ago when you had all your pimples and wore dirty clothes.'

He smiled his own love into her sparkling blue eyes. 'Well then, you should be able to understand how much I love you now, even with your burns.'

As he kissed her again, Bonnie knew she had never known such love before, nor such confusion and helplessness at her own emotions. It wouldn't be easy and there was more healing yet to come, but God was in control. The storm in her heart had calmed to a gentle breeze. Always moving, always changing, but no longer restless and wild; no longer running or being chased. In listening to God's voice and surrendering to Him she had found peace and purpose beyond all she could have imagined.

Book 2 Aussie Sky Series
Release 2014
Beauty Clements hates her name – along with everything and everyone. What will it take to get through to her? Can God's love and forgiveness free her from her past?

Book 3 Aussie Sky Series

Release 2015

Prince Clements captured Rachel's heart the moment he left the circus and rode into her school. But she is a minister's daughter and Prince has no time for God.

Book 4 Aussie Sky Series
Release 2015
Roy can't work out if clumsy Misty Clements is clever and manipulative or if she is just as lost in the world as she seems. What is she hiding from him?